CASTING THE FIRST SHADOW

Sarah looked at me despondently. I noticed that she had not moved from the kitchen doorway. She seemed not to have heard me.

"I don't like it here," she said. "There's a bad feeling. As though something happened here. Something bad."

I stared at her. Sarah was not given to flights of the imagination; that was my province.

"Nonsense," I said. I felt a bit annoyed, that a shadow had come over everything so quickly. "You can't mean that."

"I do," she said. "That's what I do mean." She was keeping her voice low, as if she were afraid someone might overhear.

"Come and have your supper," I urged, wanting her to stop. I felt a shiver run down my spine. But she remained where she was, my wife, in that old kitchen doorway.

"You haven't listened," she said. "I can feel it. I felt it upstairs just now. There's something terrible here. In this house."

Also by Jonathan Aycliffe

Whispers in the Dark
Naomi's Room

Writing as Daniel Easterman

The Ninth Buddha
Brotherhood of the Tomb
Night of the Seventh Darkness
Name of the Beast

Available from HarperPaperbacks

The **V**anishment

JONATHAN AYCLIFFE

HarperPaperbacks
A Division of HarperCollinsPublishers

HarperPaperbacks *A Division of* HarperCollins*Publishers*
10 East 53rd Street, New York, N.Y. 10022

Cover illustration by Gerry Grace

First printing: June 1994

Printed in the United States of America

HarperPaperbacks and colophon are trademarks of HarperCollins*Publishers*

❖ 10 9 8 7 6 5 4 3 2 1

For Beth and Morris, may they never vanish

Acknowledgments

Thanks, first and foremost, to the editorial skills of Patricia Parkin, who, as always, grasped the essentials and demonstrated them to me with tact and clarity; to Karen Solem and Katie Tso in distant New York, for fresh insights and a careful assessment of the text; to my wife, Beth, for listening to the story almost nightly as it developed, for nudging me gently in the right direction, and for being there; and to Lesley Johnson and Roderick Richards for their skillful research assistance.

CHAPTER

1

SOME MEMORIES linger. As often as not, the great ones flicker and fade, while the little cling to us so hard we can feel their hands on our rough skin. It is as though they are inhabited by ghosts, for like ghosts they will not leave us.

I remember nothing of the long drive down to Cornwall. Just a road like any other, the traffic thin for the time of year, sunlight during the day turning to darkness. Yes, I do remember that—it was dark when we arrived. A summer darkness, benign and reassuring. It was a July night—the fourth, the fifth; I forget exactly which—a warm night scented with flowers.

I had followed the road faithfully, and faltered only as we reached the village. The hand-drawn map sent to me by the solicitors would not hold true. The dimensions were all askew, and the scale was hopelessly inaccurate. We found a pub two steps down from the little church, and I stepped inside to inquire.

The place was full of people drinking, the locals in one corner, visitors in another: you could tell at a glance. And it was obvious to which group I belonged as I stepped through the door. It took a while, but in the end I got the attention of the landlord, a pale man in his fifties, not a native from the sound of him, ex-army or -navy, or so it seemed.

"That's your way," he said, coming outside to set me right. "The last turning on the left. Mile and a half, two miles. You can't miss it."

I could hear the sea already, a steady throbbing just on the edge of hearing. A lonely sound, coming to us as it did out of the darkness. As though, beyond the inland warmth, something cold lay in waiting.

"I expect we'll see more of you," I said. "We've booked the house for the next two months."

"I daresay," he said. And as I walked slowly back to the parked car: "Take care." I thought it queer then, or overly polite.

Sarah was waiting. She had her window down and was taking in great gulps of air, as though she hadn't breathed in months.

"Can you smell it?" she asked as I climbed back into my seat.

"What?"

"The sea. It's out there somewhere."

"I know. You can hear it if you listen hard."

And she did hear it. Her hand reached out to stop me restarting the engine, then she took my fingers in hers and held me very still.

"Everything's going to be all right, isn't it?" she whispered. In the darkness I nodded. I leaned in toward her, kissing her lightly on the cheek.

"I think we'll be happy here," I said.

She did not answer at once, but I felt her beside me, tense with excitement. I pictured her on our honeymoon, beside another sea, walking among flowers and laughing. That had been years ago. I caressed her hair lightly with my free hand.

She turned her face from the sea and kissed me, gently at first, then suddenly hard.

"I love you," she whispered.

My hand touched her cheek. I kissed her again, carefully, and smiled, though I knew she could not see me.

"Like old times," I said.

I turned the key and we crept forward into the night.

Tredannack was the nearest village to the house. It had all the normal village conveniences: a pub, a church, a general store and post office, a craft-shop-cum-tearoom run by a young widow from Penzance. We passed through what there was of the place in about ten seconds, then found ourselves on the narrow, tree-bordered road that led to Petherick House.

Petherick House. It was a childhood dream come true. As a boy, I had been taken often to St. Ives for the holidays. My parents had been amateur painters and had gone there for summer schools several years in a row, taking me with them as extra baggage. But I had loved the town, with its winding, hilly streets and its bustling harbor. In the course of excursions into the countryside to paint or picnic, we had passed by Petherick House quite often. It had impressed itself on my boyish mind as a sort of haven, a hideaway that must be inhabited by beautiful and mysterious people, people who lived glamorous lives behind tall gates.

I forgot it later. From the age of thirteen, I never returned to St. Ives, and in time most memories of the place were wiped out. And then, the previous year, while passing by on my way to a writing weekend in a remote Cornish village, I saw Petherick House again and stopped. It was not memory that stopped me, for it was only as I drove away that all those earlier impressions came flooding back. No, something else had drawn my attention. Not the house itself so much as the view it commanded over the sea, and the woods and gardens that grew half-wild all about it. It had a deserted look. And when I looked at the weather-beaten nameplate high up on one gatepost, I remembered.

It was quite by chance—or so I thought—that Sarah decided a year later that she wanted to spend the summer in the West Country, in order to paint. We tried all the usual places, but it was already late, and we found ourselves unable to get a suitable property to rent. All the National Trust and English Heritage houses had been taken months before, the prettiest cottages had gone to the families who took them every year, the few available places had revealed their drawbacks after a little astute questioning—a caravan site next door, a factory at the bottom of the lane, year-round damp.

Property after property was crossed off our list as unavailable during July, or unbookable for a two-month stretch, or in some other way unsuitable. So it was that my thoughts returned with growing insistence to the image of that empty house standing like a beacon facing the sea. Childhood dreams returned to tell me that this was the very place.

An inquiry to the tourist board at St. Ives led me to the local library, and from there I was referred to a firm of solicitors in Fore Street. They acted as agents for the house's owner, a retired gentleman living in another part of the country; it was their function to keep his property in a state of good repair, both internally and externally, and to have it inspected at regular intervals for signs of damp, rats, or squatters.

A young man called Medawar spoke to me on the telephone: the senior partner who normally dealt with the house was away, but he had authority to act in his absence. It seemed that Petherick House was not normally rented, but the owner had given the firm a very free hand, and he could see no reason not to let me have it. He named a rent which I found perfectly reasonable, and I at once agreed to his terms. That afternoon I forwarded the whole two months' rent to St. Ives, receiving in return a key and the rough map of which I have spoken.

The house was, strictly speaking, conspicuously larger than our modest needs demanded. It had seven bedrooms, four bathrooms, and a host of cupboards, cubbyholes, and closets. However, any disadvantage occasioned by its size was well compensated for by several factors. For one thing, there was that modest rent. For another, the house was well off the beaten track, hence out of the range of tourists and picnickers. Not only that, but it was remote enough even from its own village to allow us the measure of privacy we craved.

We had both brought work, even though the declared object of the two-month break was to unwind. Sarah was looking forward to painting in watercolors for the first time in years, I had hopes of starting work on the collection of short stories I had promised my publishers three years earlier and somehow never found time to write. Solitude would help us relax, a little work in the mornings would prevent us getting on one another's nerves. That was how we had planned things.

*   *   *

The village vanished behind a bend in the road, and we were swallowed up at once by the salt-scented darkness. Glancing in the mirror, I could see nothing behind, as though Tredannack had been no more than a dream. On either side of the road, tall trees fenced us in, abetted by thick low hedges and firmly shut gates. I drove slowly in a low gear, for the road turned like a bent corkscrew, now left, now right. We had come to a very great darkness, to a place without light of any kind, save for the momentary flash of our headlights as we swept past.

The beginning of solitude is often like that, like the shutting off of all sensation as you enter the deep sea and are parted from light and sound. Had I known then what darkness, what deep waters we were entering, I should have turned round and driven back in search of light forever.

The road seemed to go on for miles, far more than the one or two the landlord at the inn had predicted. I began to think that after all, I had made a wrong turn on leaving the village and must now be headed in quite the wrong direction. There were no other cars. There was no sign of life anywhere.

I had almost decided to stop and turn around when, without warning, the sign leaped out at me from the hedgerow: a square white board bearing black painted letters stained by the sea air. PETHERICK HOUSE.

"Here we are," I said, predictably.

Sarah just nodded. She had been quiet ever since we left the village. As though silenced by our entry into the dark. I knew better than to probe her mood.

My key fitted the lock on the barred gate. Beyond it lay a flagged driveway speckled with weeds. I drove slowly down it, my headlights picking out rhododendrons and magnolias, their shiny leaves glistening in the light as though wet. They were past their flowering now. But there was a smell of chamomile in the air, and tamarisk. And beyond that the sea, pressing on us harder here.

It was with us the moment we opened the car doors. We could hear it, darkly working away somewhere out in the darkness, falling and grinding. We stepped out, stiff-limbed, trying to get our bearings. The house had shown itself to us only in patches caught by the headlights on our approach. Small mullioned windows, a heavy doorway, weathered stone, flashes of ivy against old brick, stone steps flanked by little lions, their faces much worn down.

"Look," said Sarah, clutching my arm and turning me to what she had seen. I saw nothing but the night.

"Wait," she whispered.

Moments later it came again, sheet lightning far out at sea. And this time a roll of thunder, very remote, barely audible. We watched for a while, delighted by the opening and shutting of the sky. But soon the storm passed on northward, out past the horizon, leaving only occasional flickers past the rim of dark water.

"Let's go in," I said. Sarah was still clutching my arm. She leaned against me, warm now, content. She was thinking of bright light above the waves, and I was on edge, fearful of a change in the weather, for I dislike storms.

Entering an unknown house in the dark is never easy. Doing so awakens old fears, the trepidation natural to all contact with the unpredictable. I had had the foresight to bring a flashlight, and this I used to light my way for the minute or so it took to open the door and find the light switch.

Above my head, a brass temple lantern sprang into life, casting a yellow glow on a long, unfurnished hallway. Closed doors to the left and, on the right, a plain wooden staircase whose upper half was in darkness. I shivered and took a step inside. The floor had been laid with quarry tiles on which three thin rugs had been spread in a weak concession to comfort.

Sarah followed, rubbing her hands together.

"They might have laid on some heat," she complained.

"It isn't winter," I reminded her.

"All the same. It might as well be winter. It's ice-cold in here. Those stone walls. And the sea so close. We'll have to air the bed, it's bound to be damp."

We brought our essential bags inside, leaving the rest locked in the trunk for the morning. I started exploring, switching on lights as I went. There was a meter beneath the stairs that took one-pound coins, placed there, I guessed, for the convenience of anyone who had work to do in the house. I fed it as far as it would go, to be sure we would not suddenly be deprived of light or warmth. There was a central heating system of sorts, pretty antiquated, and a hot-water tank in the kitchen.

The downstairs rooms consisted of a drawing room, a dining room, a kitchen, and a little library with shelves but no books, which latter I at once appropriated for my own use as a study. The furnishings were of that tasteless breed common to unused properties, disparate items picked up in country sales, the castoffs of widows and children come into a trivial inheritance, no two pieces quite matching, nothing worth coveting, much less stealing. Much of the furniture seemed to date from the forties or fifties, yet it had a quaintly pristine look, as though the house had been a museum.

I busied myself downstairs, seeing to the kitchen, putting supplies away in cupboards, fixing a simple meal from the canned food we had brought to see us through the first days. Sarah was upstairs in the large bedroom, the one we had named our own. It had an attached bathroom and a spacious double bed whose sheets had indeed turned out to be more than a little damp. We wondered when someone had last slept there. The other bedrooms were silent and empty, each with its bed and wardrobe and chest of drawers.

Sarah came down just as I was ready to spoon out our supper. She seemed withdrawn, pensive.

"What's wrong?" I asked. "Don't you like it? I agree it's a bit bleak, but I'm sure it will seem a lot friendlier in the morning when the sun's shining and we've got it properly warmed up."

She looked at me almost despondently, I thought. I noticed that she had not moved from the kitchen doorway. She seemed not to have heard me.

"I don't like it here," she said. "There's a bad feeling. Something feels wrong. As though something happened here. Something bad."

I stared at her. Sarah was not given to flights of the imagination; that was my province.

"Nonsense," I said. I felt a bit annoyed, that a shadow had come over everything so quickly. "You can't mean that."

"I do," she said. "That's what I do mean." She was keeping her voice low, as though afraid someone might overhear.

"Come and have your supper," I urged, wanting her to stop. I had felt a shiver run down my own spine. But she remained where she was, my wife, in that old kitchen doorway.

"You haven't listened," she said. "I can feel it. I felt it upstairs just now. There's something terrible here. In this house."

CHAPTER 2

I TOOK HER OUT to the garden. The storm had passed away completely now, and the sky had filled with stars. Such clarity. A large moon had appeared midway to the horizon. We walked down to the cliff edge. I brought the thick rug from the backseat of the car and laid it down on grass made silver by the moonlight.

We sat together, facing the sea. Now that she was outside, Sarah seemed to relax. I said nothing about her unexpected fear. She had been under a lot of strain during the past year, and I had almost expected something like this. We can get by from day to day when work forces us to keep things bottled up. But once the lid is unscrewed a little, all those pent-up feelings start coming to the surface. It had happened on holiday before.

"Thank you," she said after a while.

"What for?"

"For bringing me here. It's so peaceful."

"You're feeling better?"

"Yes, better already."

She leaned against me.

"It's so warm," she said. "Like being in Spain or Italy."

"There are palm trees not far from here," I told her. "Let's skip work tomorrow. We'll drive down to the Roseland Peninsula and pretend we're in Italy."

Straightening, she removed her sweater in a single motion.

"We can do anything we like here," she said. "Anything at all."

"What if somebody's watching?" I laughed.

"Who could be watching?"

"I don't know. There might be a poacher in the woods. Or a fishing boat down there somewhere. With fishermen."

"With binoculars!"

She laughed out loud, the first real laughter I had heard from her in a long time.

"Why don't we give the buggers something to look at, then?" I leaned across and removed her bra. Moments later we were in each other's arms, kissing with a passion I had almost forgotten was possible. As though here, in this darkness above the sea, all inhibitions had been lost. Her body was silver and soft and delightfully warm. The smell of crushed grass mingled with her perfume and the scent of the sea intoxicating me.

We fell asleep afterward, naked in the warm air. Much later, waking, we were cold, but it was enough to put on our clothes again. The moon set and the tide moved in and out again. Somewhere in the woods, a night bird called. We slept again, like children out of school. When we woke, we were surrounded by sunlight, on a high cliff above a blue sea that seemed to have no end.

I went back to the house to get breakfast. We ate outside, throwing pieces of bread to the sea gulls that came dashing in to the shore. I could not remember when I had last seen Sarah so happy.

It was a long drive to the Roseland Peninsula, but my impulse to take Sarah there had been right. Crossing the River Fal on the St. Harry ferry, she got out of the car and stood at the front, watching mesmerized as the high green bank came drifting toward us. The morning's happiness was still on her, and I began to think the change would prove permanent at last.

The peninsula is a slice of paradise pinched between the Carrick Roads and the wider waters of the English Channel. It is an enclosed world of high woodlands, sheltered creeks, and sleepy villages. At its heart lies St. Just-in-Roseland, a thirteenth- and fifteenth-century church set in the most beautiful of churchyards above a quiet tidal inlet. It was there I drove the moment we left the ferry.

For the next three hours we walked hand in hand among graves and flowers, shaded by tall, semitropical trees, along paths dappled with ferns. Set down in the middle of such lush vegetation, the little stone church looked out of place, a very English building in what seemed a foreign field. But the names on the lichen-covered graves and the inscriptions on the little stones that flanked the paths could not have been more English.

We sat beneath a tall Lebanon cedar, watching the sun shift on the deep water of the creek. I had brought sandwiches and coffee for lunch. Sometimes the voices of other visitors would drift across to us, then the silence would close in again. A chaffinch flew past and landed softly on the branch of a tall myrtle. There were birds everywhere. The air was full of birdsong and the buzzing of bees. Butterflies danced in pools of sunlight.

"How wonderful if I could be buried here," whispered Sarah. She was leaning back against my chest with her eyes closed. I ran a slow finger back and forth across her lips. "So much nicer than . . ." She shivered.

"Well, wherever it is I'll wind up."

"I thought you were going to be cremated. And put in the jar with Brian." Brian had been our cat. He had died two years before and Sarah had kept his ashes in a biscuit tin on the mantelpiece. She said we were all to be mingled one day and sprinkled on Hampstead Heath.

"Well, we could be sprinkled here, I suppose."

"I'm not sure they'd take very kindly to having a cat on their roses."

"They needn't know."

"A heathen, then. You might contaminate the place."

"It was just a thought. I almost envy them all." She glanced up the hill at the old graves. "Being part of this. Sleeping here."

There was nothing morbid in her tone. Just a subdued awe to find that death could be turned into such a gentle thing. I knew what she was thinking, though. She was thinking about Catherine, our daughter, about her small flower-covered grave in London. It seemed so long ago now. So long ago, so sudden, so unnecessary.

I stopped thinking about it. If Sarah could find comfort here, so could I. It was only a matter of making room.

We finished our lunch and took another slow walk,

returning at last to the creek, where we sat by the water's edge. Sarah talked about returning here to paint. I had brought my camera. We took photographs of each other. I have them still. We are happy in them, smiling, content with life.

We spent the late afternoon in Falmouth and had dinner there. It was late when we finally got back. We were greeted by the sound of the sea and the silent, shadowed shape of Petherick House against the night sky. We were ready for our first night inside.

CHAPTER 3

I DID WHAT I COULD to keep Sarah's spirits high. I found wood in an outhouse and succeeded in lighting a fire in our drab bedroom. The flames made the room almost cheerful, and the warmth was welcome, driving away as it did some of that unseasonal cold and damp. It seemed hard to believe that we had spent the day in such glorious summer weather.

"I want to go home," Sarah said when she came upstairs, before we undressed for bed.

"Home? But I thought you'd got over that."

"I thought so as well. But I can't stay here. Truly I can't."

"What's wrong with it? Really. Other than this . . . feeling?"

"I don't know. Don't you see, that's the problem? I feel this way, and I know I shouldn't, and it unsettles me."

"Well, it may not be so bad in the morning. You're

tired. It's been a long day. We can go back to Roseland anytime you want."

"Perhaps," she said, but I could see she was not convinced. Her hair was dark, the color of polished wood, and she let it fall over her shoulders like a shawl. I reached out my hand and touched it. It was soft.

Several times that night I woke and found Sarah awake in the bed beside me, first on her back, then on her side, now upright.

"Can't you sleep?"

She took her time answering. In the interval, I could hear the sea rolling outside.

"No," she said. "I keep thinking. I can't stop thinking about it."

"It?"

"The house. About this house. I think about one room, then the next, until I've been through them all. And then I start again, all over, from the beginning."

"You should try sheep instead."

"It isn't funny, Peter. Something happened here. In one of these rooms."

After that, I did not sleep either. Dawn found us still in bed, wide-awake, like children on Christmas morning. The fire had died out.

Sometimes, there are more dreams than I can bear. Sometimes, the night is thick with them, so thick I wake choking and am taken down again in wave after wave of breathlessness. In time, I recover wakefulness and pull myself upright in bed, for I know I cannot sleep again. Or, rather, that I will not. I prefer not to, I know what I will encounter if I do. You can hear things in dreams, see things, touch things—things best left alone, things best forgotten.

*   *   *

There was bright sun all that day again. We break-
fasted early to the sound of birds. The central heating had begun to make an impact on the rooms,
taking the chill off the air. Throughout the meal I
steered what little conversation there was on to
neutral topics—places I thought we should put on
our itinerary, the prospects for good weather,
whether or not we should go shopping for fresh
food that afternoon. Tired of my own voice, I
switched on the radio. A deejay was babbling mind-
lessly on Radio One, but his cheery voice and the
undemanding music he played were exactly what
we needed.

After breakfast, we went straight out to the garden.
Sarah's mood lifted almost at once, returning to what
it had been the day before. It was already warm outside, and sunlight had woven itself into everything. At
the rear of the house, a daisy-speckled lawn ran gently
down to the cliff, at whose foot the sea lay, breathing
dangerously. A scattering of jagged rocks guarded the
cliff face against the waves, as though dropped there
on purpose.

We stood at the edge together, holding hands,
watching the tide come in. The house stood behind
us, not quite forgotten, but pushed aside for a while.
The rug still lay where we had left it. An army of sea
gulls dipped and soared around us, lifting from the
wrinkled surface of the waves, turning and vanish-
ing into the blue sky. I drew back from the edge,
made nervous by the beating of the sea against those
black, glistening rocks. Sarah followed me without a
word.

I found two folding chairs and set them on the
lawn, a white table between. On the table I placed a

jug of fruit juice and ice, with glasses. Sarah said nothing more about leaving, or about her feelings of the night before, and I did not prompt her.

We took lunch on the lawn: tuna and corned-beef sandwiches washed down with hot coffee. Afterward, Sarah stretched out on a recliner and fell asleep, exhausted by the night's vigil. Curiously, I did not feel tired, but invigorated, woken up by the sun and the sea breeze. I was like someone who has spent years in solitary confinement, who has not felt the sun on his face or smelled fresh air for almost as long as he can remember. I brought a pen and paper from the car and made a start on a story I had been mulling over on the way down.

I surprised myself. By the time I put the pen down, it was midafternoon and I had written half a dozen pages. I reread them and was pleased to find the results better than I had expected. The best thing I had written in ages. The real thing for once.

At that moment Sarah woke up screaming.

The sound ripped me from my reading. She was sitting bolt upright on the recliner, eyes open, staring, hands thrust out as though to ward off an unseen attacker. I knocked back my chair as I stood and rushed to her side.

"Sarah, what is it? Are you all right?"

She looked at me for a moment as though she did not recognize me, then took three or four deep breaths and lowered her hands to the base of the recliner, pressing hard against it for balance. I reached out for her, touching her gently, though I sensed on her part a reluctance to be touched.

"It was a dream," she said. "I had a dream."

At that moment she looked around toward the house. I saw her shiver as she did so. By ill chance, a cloud chose that instant to cross the sun, sending a streak of dark shadow across the lawn and down onto the rear of the building.

"We have to go," she said. "We have to leave."

"Leave?" I retorted, as though stung. "We can't leave. There's no question of leaving."

"You don't understand. It's what I said. The house—"

"There's nothing wrong with the house, Sarah. This place is all we expected. Sunny, quiet, restful. I've done more work this afternoon than I've sometimes done in an entire month in London. Better work, too. At this rate I'll have the book half finished by the time we go home."

"No, Peter, we have to go now. Before something happens."

"Happens? Nothing's going to happen. You're just frightening yourself for nothing. You can paint if you like, go for walks, get a boat—whatever you like. But I'm staying here to write. Every day if I can."

"Then I'll go home alone."

I took my hand away from her, the hand with which I had been stroking her shoulders.

"Fine," I said. "Do that." I hesitated, knowing that what I said next would be crucial, a watershed perhaps. "But don't expect me to come after you. Not now, not later. Do you understand?"

She understood. Whatever the dream had done to her, my words went deeper. I was offering her a choice, a bastard choice. She could let her fears get the better of her, slip away to London, escape whatever it was she dreaded here, but it would be the beginning of the end of our marriage. Or she could decide to save the marriage by staying here and fighting it. It was a cruel choice, and I am not proud of having forced it on her. Not in view of what happened later. But I had no way of knowing. Not then.

She said nothing. All her energies were reserved for

the struggle going on inside her. Partly, it was a struggle with the house; partly, one with me. I won, or at least I was given the appearance of winning. Sarah got up and walked down to the lawn's edge, where she sat for a long time, watching the sea. A boat went slowly past, a red smudge against the waves.

That night I worked late in the study, making rapid progress with my story. It would be finished by the next day if all went well.

Sarah was in the drawing room, painting. She had brought daylight bulbs and set up lamps alongside her easel. I was under strict orders not to enter the room while she was working. My scrutiny made her nervous, she said. I was happy to comply.

I stopped work at eleven. Sarah was already in the kitchen, preparing hot drinks. She seemed more relaxed. On reflection, I understood in part her sense of unease concerning the house. It was, after all, far from the most cheerful of dwellings, even in this, its modern phase. How it might have been fifty or one hundred years ago, I shuddered to imagine. And in the winter it must be bleak enough, its rooms permanently chilled, touched with damp.

There were three stories. Downstairs consisted of the rooms I have mentioned, and there was also a toilet. The next floor had four bedrooms, including our own, and two bathrooms; the remaining three bedrooms were on the upper story, with two smaller bathrooms. Old carpet, old wallpaper everywhere: the house had not been redecorated since the 1950s or earlier. Our bedroom looked out onto the garden at the back, and to the sea beyond. The bed creaked. A tap in the bathroom dripped.

We went to bed around midnight. I was tired at last, yet buoyed up by my achievements of the day.

"How did your painting go?" I asked as we settled into bed.

"Well. Very well. As you say, this is a good place to work. Things get done."

"I'm pleased. But today wasn't much of a success, was it? I thought things were going well yesterday."

She was silent for a while.

"You've got some work done. It's what you wanted."

"Nevertheless."

I stroked her cheek. The sheets were still a little damp, but Sarah's body beside me was warm, even hot. My hand stroked her flank, and I felt her go rigid briefly, then relax. I continued stroking, and she sighed audibly. The sheet slipped down below her breasts, and I leaned over, kissing her. She did not try to stop me.

It was not like that last time, on the lawn. Sarah kept her eyes shut from start to finish. Outside, she had been free of all inhibition; here, it was as if we were being watched or overheard.

Afterward, we listened to the sea. I imagined it in the darkness, always moving. Not melodic as before, but out of tune and sinister.

Sarah held my hand.

"I've been here before," she said.

The words were almost a whisper. I asked her what she meant. But she did not answer. She let go of my hand and turned on her side and switched off the light.

When I woke later that night, she was sitting upright again. I did not ask what she was doing. I knew. In her mind, she was making her way from room to room, all through the silent house.

CHAPTER 4

DAY FOLLOWED DAY, night succeeded night, and the weather did not change, did not even falter. Each day Sarah took her easel down to the cliff edge, where she painted endlessly, sometimes from early morning to late afternoon, without flagging. The finished products of her labor were stored under sheets in one of the second-floor bedrooms. She promised to reveal them only when we were back in London. It would be a surprise, she said, part of my homecoming.

I wrote as I had never written before. Each morning I typed up the work of the previous day, refining and editing it, and each afternoon, after a brief rest outside in the garden, I would take up my pen again and write ten, eleven, twelve pages without so much as a pause. I worked in the study for the most part, seated in front of a French window that gave onto the garden. Old, discarded ideas were taken out and dusted off; in the peace and quiet of those golden days, they quickly came back to life. I felt as though I had become a magician, as though all I touched was in a matter of moments gold. I had never written so well or so easily, and every day I woke anxiously, fearing that the facility might have left me as readily as it had come, only to find it waiting there in the study, quietly, without fail.

In the soft evenings, Sarah and I would drive in to Tredannack, to the Green Dragon pub. The landlord recognized me and made us welcome. I soon learned that he was not a local, but a Plymouth man, a former sailor who had retired early and come to Tredannack with a young wife, to indulge a long-postponed dream of life as a country innkeeper.

There were a few outsiders like ourselves, summer folk who rented cottages in the village or parked their caravans nearby. They came from Birmingham and Manchester, sunless northern towns, and we found them a dull bunch on the whole. Back home, they sold cars or insurance or double glazing, and their conversation was limited to house prices, the crime rate, and the tribulations of the Royal Family, of whom they spoke with the familiarity of close friends.

From long experience, I knew better than to let myself be drawn into the subject of my own work. I said what I always say, that I was a civil servant—something I had indeed been at one time—and mentioned a dull department on the third floor of an office in Brentford. No one inquired further. I was a pencil pusher, one of the innumerable faceless minions to whom their forms and reports were passed.

By the third evening, we had decided to progress to the locals, only to find ourselves met by a blank wall. They were not overtly rude—not at first—but they made it wholly clear that they wanted nothing to do with us. Now at one table, now at another, we were snubbed again and again, and in the end we stopped trying and settled for our own company. I thought at first it was no more than the usual and forgivable resistance of residents to contact with seasonal visitors. But from time to time I would catch sight of one of our friends from the north playing darts with a team of local lads or ordering a round for one or another circle of Tredannack worthies. If there was a ban, it started and ended with us.

There was no alternative to the Green Dragon. It was all the pub and all the nightlife in the whole of Tredannack, and for what it was worth, we felt ourselves entitled to some company in the evenings. It kept Sarah away from the house for one thing, and I was grateful for that. And the beer was good, a heady local brew that made a fitting end to a hard day's writing. I had started to look forward to it.

So we sat it out for two more nights. From time to time we would notice eyes straying in our direction, then away again. We had not become invisible, then. New arrivals entering the lounge would glance around, spying out their friends; without fail, their eyes would rest on us for a moment or two, warily, before moving on.

Late on the second evening of cold shoulders and odd looks—our fifth at the pub—I went up to the bar to fetch fresh drinks for us both: another pint of Polyphant's Old Cornish Regular for myself, a Tanqueray gin for Sarah. The landlord served me as usual, but I thought he, too, glanced at me oddly. I could hold back no longer.

"What is it, Ted?" I asked. "People have been treating us like lepers for the past two nights. Don't tell me we've got BO."

He set the brimming pint glass on the bar and turned to fetch a tumbler for Sarah's gin.

"They're odd buggers round here," he said, keeping his voice low. "I'd pay no heed to them if I were you."

"But I can't help paying heed. They give us queer glances, they make it clear we're pariahs of some sort."

"You're from outside. I had a hard enough time of it myself when I first came here."

"Don't give me that," I said. "Look at them. They're happy enough to pass the time of day with that riffraff from the caravans. Don't tell me they've got a special phobia of Londoners."

He filled the gin glass with tonic.

"Ice?"

"Yes, please."

He spooned some in and added a wedge of lemon. I passed a five-pound note across the bar and he gave me my change.

"It's not you," he said. "It's the house you're staying in. Some local thing. I can't get to the bottom of it. People clam up if you mention it."

"What about the house?" I was sure he knew more than he said. "What's wrong with it?"

But I knew myself, of course I did. Sarah had told me already.

He shook his head.

"I don't know," he said. "Really I don't. Just forget I said anything." I did not believe him, but I saw there was no point in pressing. He had lived in Tredannack too long, had become a local himself. And he had to stay on here long after Sarah and I would have gone. I left him to his beer pumps and took my drinks back to our table.

Sarah was not there. I looked around, but she was nowhere in sight. I guessed she had gone to the toilet, so I sat down to wait for her.

She did not reappear until I was over halfway through my pint. Most of the ice in her glass had melted. I saw her come through the lounge door, followed closely by a local woman, of whom all I knew was that her name was Margaret.

"Where have you been?" I asked. She looked pale and a little seedy. One glaring thought came into my head, but I pushed it out again quickly. Sarah hadn't taken tranquilizers in years, wasn't likely to start again in a place like Tredannack.

"Let's get out of here, Peter. I've had enough for one evening."

I could sense the strain in her voice.

"What's wrong? Don't you want your gin? I'll get a fresh one if you like."

"I've had enough to drink. Come on, let's go. I'll drive if you aren't up to it."

"No, I'm okay."

I picked up my beret and put it on. It was a recent affectation, and I clung to it tenaciously. Before leaving, I gulped down the rest of my pint. I would miss it when it was time to go home.

Outside, the weather had changed. There was a chill in the air. A sense of impending rain, perhaps a storm. Something charged and angry in the atmosphere. I could feel it. Something was coming. I shivered as I got into the car.

Sarah turned to me and blurted out what was troubling her.

"Peter, we can't stay in the house."

"Oh, God. Not that again."

"No, not that, not like before. This is different. Margaret Trebarvah told me why the locals won't have anything to do with us. It's not us at all—"

"It's the house. I know. Ted Bickleigh told me much the same thing."

"Did he tell you why?"

"No. It's some great local secret."

"Margaret told me a little. I think she knows more, but she can't tell or won't. What she did say was enough, though. I was right about the house. Something terrible did happen there. Margaret didn't know the details, or she wouldn't tell me, but she knows that someone was murdered there and that they refuse to leave, refuse to believe they're dead."

"So that's all it comes to in the end," I said. "A common or garden ghost. How very sad."

"Don't make fun of it, Peter. Even if you can't feel it yourself, you know I sensed it the moment we arrived. There's one room. One room where all the evil in the house is concentrated. Haven't you even felt it a little?"

I ignored her question.

"And if there is a ghost?" I snorted. "We haven't seen or heard anything. It seems willing to leave us alone. Let's leave it like that."

"You don't understand, do you, Peter? It doesn't leave us alone. It's always there. It watches us when we sleep. Sometimes when I wake up, I know it's there. Watching. Waiting. I don't know what for."

I started the car.

"This is ridiculous, Sarah. You're letting a hysterical woman frighten you. Maybe these people have their reasons for scaring visitors off, God knows. But I'm damned if I'll let them do it to me."

Sarah fell silent. She knew better than to argue when I was in that mood, knew that anything she might say would fall on deaf ears or, worse, provoke me to a rage. I am not always even-tempered when I drink, and that night I had downed enough Old Cornish Regular to awaken a few demons. I drove back faster than was safe, with my lights on full beam, skimming hedgerows, and several times I came close to planting us in a ditch.

The house was waiting for us, quiet beneath a growing moon. Sarah came in behind me, more reluctant than ever. The black mood was leaving me, exorcised by the drive. I apologized for my outburst in the car, but Sarah only nodded and said nothing; she knew how little it would take to set me off a second time. It felt chilly, almost as cold as on that first night. I got the central heating on full again and lit the Aga stove in the kitchen. Sarah stayed with me. I made sandwiches and cocoa, and we ate in silence. As though we were listening.

Much later, in bed, I sat up reading. Beside me, Sarah had fallen into an uneasy sleep. From time to time she stirred, twice she cried out gently. I touched her arm, soothing her. She meant a great deal to me. Not everything, nobody means that much; but the thought of separation terrified me. I regretted my impatience. I bent and kissed her, hoping she might sense my contrition in her dreams. Tonight I could not sleep myself. A wind had risen and was pushing hard across the sea. There was a tremendous sense of change in the air, as though nature was in flux. I returned to my book, but I could not concentrate. Rain had started to fall. I could hear it hissing against the windows, not loud, but insistent nonetheless. It sounded desolate, a rain of long distances, of empty places.

I could not sleep. The wind and the rain and my own thoughts prevented it. About two o'clock, I gave up the struggle and slipped out of bed. That evening, I had left a story half-finished; sleeplessness had more or less completed it for me, and I wanted to get it down on paper while my thoughts were still fresh. I knew I should not sleep until I did so. I dressed in the dark and went downstairs. Sarah did not stir.

The study was cold. I lit the electric fire and sat

down at my desk, rubbing my hands together. It was
not, I thought, so much cold as a memory of cold.
What that meant I could not then have said, though I
might now. Everything leaves its trace.

The room was ill lit. Little shadows clung to the
walls. I went straight to work. The compulsion to
write was on me with as much strength as ever.

Outside, the rain continued, growing in intensity as
the night progressed. The wind, too, kept rising, and I
fancied I could hear waves dashing against the cliff.
Inside, the sounds were muffled. From time to time
something would bang or rattle. I would look up occa-
sionally at some creak or scratch, then bend back to my
writing. When I first looked at the clock, it was nearly
three. By the time I looked again, it was half past.

I leaned back and stretched. The story was almost
finished. I was starting to grow drowsy, but I determined to get to the end before going back to bed. I
yawned and leaned forward again. That was when I
noticed that something was wrong, that something
had changed, though I did not know what. The wind
and rain had stopped while I was writing. The night
was silent. A great stillness held everything, and the
house seemed to be unnaturally without sound.

For a moment I was sure I had heard someone
breathing. I would have to get out of Sarah whatever
it was that the interfering Margaret had told her. Not
far to go now, I would be finished by four.

Suddenly, the fire and the lights went out. I swore,
realizing I had omitted to feed the meter that morning,
not knowing it would grow cold later. I had left my
tiny reading lamp in the bedroom. There was nothing
for it but to grope my way to the meter in the dark. I
scraped my chair back and began to make my way
across the room. It was pitch-dark, I could see absolutely nothing. And in spite of the warmth that had

been generated by the fire, it had grown cold again suddenly.

I must have been about halfway across the room, very nearly at the door, when I heard a voice behind me, a woman's voice, not Sarah's, low yet distinct. Only one word was spoken, a name: "Catherine."

I spun around.

"Who's there?" I demanded.

No one answered.

"Who's there?" I said again.

Still no reply.

There was a sound of footsteps, quick, running footsteps in the hall. My eyes had by now grown a little better accustomed to the dark, and I could make out, if only with the greatest difficulty, the rough contours of the room in which I stood. I hurried to the door and flung it open.

A little moonlight crept into the hall through the transom window. I could see no one there or on the stairs. None of the downstairs doors were open, with the exception of the one I had just stepped through. This time I did not call out.

I found the meter under the stairs and hurried to cram it with the pound coins I had been carrying in my pocket. The lights in the hall and study came on again at once. Nervously, I went back to the study and looked inside: there was no one there. Behind me, the hall was still empty.

For no good reason, I felt suddenly anxious about Sarah. I had left her alone in the bedroom for longer than I should have done. What if she had wakened, brought out of sleep by the wind or the rain, or more gently by their ceasing, and found me gone? Considering her fear of the house, I knew she might well have been panic-stricken. Had those been her feet in the passage just now?

I climbed the stairs quietly, not wishing to waken her if she was still asleep. The lights did not flicker, but I felt an unaccountable fear lest they dim or cut out again. The sound of the woman's voice calling "Catherine" was still ringing in my head, I could hear it as plainly as if it had just been uttered, and I was sure it had been real. It had brought back difficult memories.

The silence was so strong, I longed for the wind and rain to return, for some sound other than my own breathing to be there beside me. I opened the bedroom door gently and stepped inside, letting a little light from the landing fall through. It was enough to see by. Enough to see that the bed was empty. I switched on the main light. Sarah was not there.

CHAPTER 5

NOR WAS SHE in the bathroom. I called loudly, going back on to the landing. I thought she might have gone up to the room where her paintings were kept, and I went there. It was empty, too. Calling her name, I went through the house room by silent room. I did not find Sarah in any of them. They were cold and unwelcoming. It was as though she had vanished into thin air. I began to grow afraid. As yet I did not really know what I was frightened of. My heart was beating unpleasantly. My hands felt clammy and unwashed. I told myself she had only gone for a walk.

I went straight outside. The car was there, of course, as I had known it would be. If Sarah had taken it, I would have heard the engine starting up, seen the headlights as it turned to go down the drive. I reckoned that she must have called a cab from St. Ives, notwithstanding the lateness of the hour. Then I realized that I would have heard and seen that, too. Which meant that she must be on foot.

Pausing only to fetch the keys, I got in the car and drove down to the main road, where I turned left for Tredannack. My guess was that she would have headed that way. Having no precise idea as to when she had wakened or how soon after that decided to leave, I could only guess how far she might have gone. She might just have reached the village, though I thought it highly unlikely. And just what she intended to do there in the middle of the night was anybody's guess.

The road was empty and melancholy. It swooped through shadows into yet more shadows. I drove slowly, afraid I might hit Sarah if she was on the wrong side wearing her dark raincoat. Hedgerows flashed past on either side, and I kept turning my gaze from right to left, not knowing where she might be. Twice, rabbits stood at the roadside, frozen in my headlights, and once a fox ran out from the cover of a ditch. But of Sarah there was no sign.

Almost without realizing it, I saw that I had arrived at the outskirts of the village. I drove down the main street slowly, but Sarah was still nowhere to be seen. The houses and shops lay huddled in a uniform darkness. The pub was shut up. A handful of dim streetlights illuminated the narrow pavements, still wet and glistening with rain.

Dispirited, I drove slowly back, then five or six miles west, in the Land's End direction. I gave up when I came to a crossroads and had no means of guessing which fork to take. I was warm by now, but outside, the countryside was still wet and cold. To the east, a faint light had started to touch the edges of the sky. I drove back to Petherick House in low spirits.

The same lights were on that had been shining

when I left. I called loudly, but still no one replied. I began for the first time to feel a sense of apprehension. For all I knew, she was out in the garden somewhere, shivering in the dawn breeze, thinking things over. She had her moods, as I had mine, and she would often take to isolation as a means of escape.

I climbed the stairs to the bedroom. I felt exhausted, drained of energy. More people die at dawn than at any other time of day. The atmosphere is thinned out then, the spirit is at its weakest. Drained, etiolated, almost without substance.

None of the suitcases or bags had been touched. I looked in the wardrobe: all Sarah's clothes were there, as far as I could see. Her underwear was in its drawer. Her makeup stood on the dressing table. I found that reassuring, for it all suggested that she planned to return, that she had merely wanted to be out of the house for one night.

I switched off the lights downstairs and returned to bed. The sheets were cold. Damp had returned, making the bed unpleasant to lie in. Outside the window, still dimmed by the curtains, daylight was seeping across the wet world. I lay with my eyes tightly shut, trying to calm my thoughts enough to sleep. The bed would not grow warm. I turned, now onto my right side, now onto my left, then I tried sitting upright. Two things above all troubled my thoughts and kept sleep far away: the sound of feet running quickly in the downstairs passage, a strange woman's voice calling "Catherine" with great distinctness.

Once or twice I opened my eyes involuntarily and looked around at the ill-proportioned room, just visible in the pale morning light. I half expected to see Sarah standing there, watching me, though why she would have come back to watch me like that I could not have said.

In the end, exhaustion got the better of me. Without quite knowing it, I dreamed I was in the corridor outside our bedroom. Something about the house had changed, though I was unable to say exactly what. I was listening for something. Or someone. On either side of me, the doors to the other rooms on the first floor stood open, but all the interiors were in darkness, and I could not see farther than the doors.

Suddenly there was a sound of light footsteps behind me, approaching slowly. I tried to turn, to face whoever was approaching me, but to my horror found I could not move my neck, and that my feet were rooted to the floor. The next moment there was a series of ear-shattering crashes as the doors in the house slammed shut—first those on the first floor, where I was, then those above, and finally those underneath.

The last bang woke me. I was sitting bolt upright and was sweating profusely. I looked anxiously around the room, but it was still empty. The daylight had grown in strength, though it was still considerably dulled by the thick curtains.

On my second attempt, I realized that sleep was impossible. I could not sleep, and I did not want to. The dream had left a foul sense of uneasiness. I half expected to hear the doors in the house bang shut in succession as they had done in my imaginings. Abandoning even the urge to sleep, I climbed out of bed again and dressed. It was just after seven o'clock.

Sarah had not come back. There was no sign of her in any of the downstairs rooms. I made a hot breakfast, washed down with three cups of strong black coffee. From time to time I found myself listening for footsteps. Sarah's footsteps, or so I told myself. There were no others, could not have been any others.

Sarah's straw hat was not on the nail on the back of the door where she had hung it every evening on coming in from the garden. I looked around, but it was nowhere in the kitchen. It puzzled me that she should have taken it with her, when she had left everything else behind.

Fortified by breakfast, I went out to the garden. The grass was still wet from the night before, but the sun was steadily growing stronger, and it looked set for a return of the fine weather. At least that would lift Sarah's spirits, I thought. Every so often I looked up, expecting to see her coming across the lawn, wearing her straw hat and smiling.

I strolled down to the cliff edge, where she normally painted. There was no sign of her. There were five or six acres of grounds altogether, much of them covered in trees and bushes. I made a thorough search of the entire area, but nowhere could I find a trace of Sarah. Now I started to grow anxious again. If she was not in the house and not in the gardens, if she had not been on the road to Tredannack or the road leading in the opposite direction, where on earth could she be?

There was one unpleasant possibility that I did my best to banish from my thoughts. But it kept nagging me until I could no longer ignore it. I made my way back to the cliff, and this time I looked deliberately and apprehensively over its edge, to the rocks below. A great sense of relief swept over me. There was nothing there. Sarah had not stumbled to her death in the dark.

All day I waited, but she did not return. Somehow, she had given me the slip—stayed in the garden, perhaps, until she saw me leave, waited for my return from Tredannack, then set off in that direction after all. It all seemed so calculated, so calculating—that was the only problem. It was not in Sarah's nature to think things out like that, coldly, step-by-step. She was intuitive, given to impulses, never deliberate. And if her departure from the house had been as precipitate as I guessed, I could see little likelihood of her having hung about merely to play a trick on me.

She could be anywhere by now, I thought. Most likely she was on her way to London and would ring me when she got there. The first trains from Penzance to Paddington arrived at 10:00, 11:45, and 1:40. The times were printed in the timetable we had brought with us in case one or the other might need to go back in a hurry without the car. I had thought to bring it; as I say, I was always the provident one.

After each of the times a train was due, I waited for the phone to ring. We had rented a cellular for two months, knowing there would be none in the house and not wanting to be wholly incommunicado. I did not sit by it like a worried parent, but I waited nonetheless. It did not ring.

The day passed, marked invisibly by these points of possible connection between Sarah and myself. There was a long gap between the 3:00 arrival and the next, at 7:43. I had started to grieve inwardly by now, though I kept telling myself it was much too early for that. All the same, I knew her strength of spirit, her ability to make a decision when she had to, her tenacity in sticking to it once it had been reached. If she had left me this time, bringing her back would not prove easy; I knew that with the dull, aching certainty of the newly bereaved. But I had seen no corpse, no farewell letter, no concrete indication that she intended to leave me.

From time to time I tried to write, but the thing was not on me, not that day, not for some time after. My thoughts were constantly torn apart by speculation about Sarah, above all the vexed question of whether she had decided to walk out on me or not. She had done it twice before, but only for short periods, and each time she had left a note saying where she was going.

I did not go down to Tredannack that evening, to the pub. There was the possibility that the phone might ring while I was absent. I listened to the radio for a while, a program about Russian icons. An old man spoke in a measured voice of tempera and gesso, of levkas and gold. Images of saints with stern faces and gilded halos fell like so many drops of water on my numbed brain. The telephone did not ring. I tried it out once, just to make sure it was working. The engineers assured me that it was in perfect order, and rang me back to prove it.

There were people in London I thought of phoning, friends who might know if she was back. I rang our flat there several times, but the reply was from the answering machine. On two occasions I left a brief message, asking Sarah to ring me if she did arrive home. I realized that she had left her handbag behind. Unless she had taken cash, she would not have had enough money to get to London.

It grew dark sometime after nine o'clock. A curious darkness, not summerlike, but harsher, denser, more complete. It had grown warmer throughout the day, but now, with the sun down again, the warmth in the air vanished rapidly, and I was forced to put the heating on again, checking first that I had fed the meter. Outside, the sea grew in volume, as though a wind were rising. There had been no forecast of storms.

It was around midnight when I heard a door slam upstairs. One of the bedroom doors. I was in the living room. The radio had been switched off, and I was trying to concentrate on Nabokov's *Pale Fire*. The sound caught me completely by surprise, making me jump. Sarah must have come in quietly, I thought, and gone straight up to our room, thinking, perhaps, that I was already there.

I waited for what must have been about five minutes, but there was no further sound upstairs. In all likelihood, Sarah was still angry with me.

I went out. The passage and staircase were in pitch darkness. I switched on lights and stood for a moment at the foot of the stairs, gazing upward as though not quite certain what I should find up there. It was cold in the passage, not a summer's night at all.

I climbed the stairs slowly. Something—instinct, an imperfect apprehension, guilt; I cannot be sure—something held me back from calling out.

I reached our bedroom door in silence. It was wide open, as I had left it, and the room itself was in darkness.

"Sarah? Are you there, love?" I said, switching on the light.

But there was no one.

I looked in each of the other rooms on that floor, but she was not in any of them. I had begun to feel afraid again. Begun to fear that it had not after all been Sarah, that I was still alone in the house, but that someone—or something—else had returned there. Someone or something that had never been away.

I climbed the steep stairs to the next floor. Three rooms, and the door to one of them wide open. It had not been open when I had been up there last. I started to say Sarah's name, but the word dried in my throat. I moved toward the room.

At that moment the door slammed hard. The sound and movement made me jump. For over a minute, I stood petrified, unable to speak or move. There was no other sound. The house was desperately quiet, as though it was waiting for something. I told myself that a draft had slammed the door, that a window must have been left open, that the rising wind had been to blame, that and nothing else.

Resisting the temptation to turn and hurry back downstairs, I stepped through the doorway and switched on the light.

An empty room. No furniture, not even a chair. It had been a bedroom once, it was large enough, and there was an old fireplace to one side, its grate blocked up. A large patch of damp sat on the wall opposite. I noticed right away that the window was firmly closed. Then I caught sight of something lying on the floor.

It was Sarah's straw hat, or what was left of it. Someone—or something—had ripped it to shreds, leaving it recognizable only by the band that still hung to the tatters of the broken crown. I stood staring rigidly at it, not understanding.

It was as I stared that I began to comprehend exactly where I was. There was a room, Sarah had said, a particular room in which the horror of the house was concentrated. I do not know how I knew— not at that moment, not then. But I did know, I knew with absolute certainty that the room I stood in was the room she had meant.

CHAPTER 6

I PASSED THAT NIGHT in very little comfort. I told myself that I had seen nothing preternatural, heard only what I had taken, perhaps wrongly, to be footsteps or the slamming of a door, imagined a voice uttering a name that had no meaning for me. Yet I could not rest entirely easy. I was assailed by uncomfortable thoughts.

Around midnight, I rang the London friends I had been meaning to ring earlier. Tim and Susan always went to bed late, I knew they would not mind. Susan came to the phone.

"Susie? This is Peter."

"Peter? What the hell are you ringing at this time for?"

"It's only midnight, Susie. Or it is down here in Cornwall."

"Well, it isn't in bloody London. It's after three in the morning here. You've probably woken Rachel. I'll never get her back to sleep."

Rachel was their daughter, a child of four.

I looked at my watch. Susie was right. What had made me think it was only midnight?

"Susie, I'm dreadfully sorry. I was sure it was only twelve. One of the clocks must have stopped or something."

"Are you all right, Peter? You don't sound yourself."

I hesitated. Susan often jumped to conclusions. She was a journalist, a professional maker of snap judgments.

"It's Sarah," I said finally. "I think she's gone back to London. Have you got her there?"

Silence for what seemed like minutes.

"Have you two quarreled again?" There was a resigned quality to her voice. "I thought you were getting it together, Peter. I thought all that was over."

"We were, we are. It's just . . . Listen, Susan, it's difficult to explain. Something frightened her, something stupid. A woman in the local pub . . . The thing is, I think she took a sudden decision to leave. I haven't heard from her since last night, but . . ."

"Well, she isn't here."

I could tell from the tone in Susan's voice that I was being blamed. If this had been some years earlier, she might have been right. I had been to blame once. But not this time.

"Have you heard from her?"

"No. I've been in all day, I would have been here if she'd rung. Have you tried ringing your own number?"

"Of course I have," I said. "I can't get anything but the answering machine. You couldn't . . ." I paused. "You couldn't pop round in the morning, could you? See if she's all right, needs anything."

"I can't, Peter. I've got a meeting all morning."

"Well, what about Tim? Could he go over, do you think?"

I sensed reluctance. They had been involved so many times in our messy lives, in our fallings-out and makings-up. I think they had looked forward to our holiday as much as we had done. And yet they were our closest, dearest friends. That had to count for something.

"I don't know, Peter. He's gone back to sleep. I'll ask him in the morning. But I know he's busy with his Lithuania project, he could be tied up all day. Why don't you get Sarah's mother to call?"

"I don't want her involved. You should know better than to suggest it. You know what she's like."

"Well, all right. I'll ask Tim."

"We haven't quarreled, Susan. Truly we haven't."

"Tell me about it tomorrow, Peter. I'll be back around one. And get your bloody clock fixed."

That night I dreamed a very strange dream. I dreamed I was in the hallway, looking up the stairs. For some reason, I was afraid. There was something at the top of the stairs, something I did not want to see or meet. And the upper half of the staircase was in darkness. In spite of my fear, I felt myself being drawn, step by reluctant step, along the hall to the foot of the stairs. I looked up into the darkness, struggling to tear myself away, but the force that drew me upward was more powerful than my fear. I started climbing the stairs. As my foot touched the first step I woke to the sound of my own voice, barking like a dog's.

I rang Susan at five past one. She reminded me that I had not given her the address for Petherick House or my phone number. When I had dictated them, I asked if there was any news.

"Tim went over this morning, Peter. He got no answer to the bell, so he let himself in. There was no sign that Sarah had been back. I tried ringing half an hour ago, but it's still the answering machine. Can you think of anywhere else she might go? Pat's, maybe?"

"Her sister, Lorna," I suggested lamely.

"Well, why don't you try her and anybody else you can think of? If you draw a blank, ring back and we'll talk it over. Tim's due back around half past five. I'll ring before that if I hear anything at all."

"I'm frightened, Susan," I said weakly.

"There's no need to be. She'll turn up. You'll see."

But that wasn't what I had meant.

By half past five I was profoundly worried. Lorna had heard nothing and was frostier than ever. I rang Sarah's mother and father in Huddersfield; they said she hadn't been in touch. Her father quizzed me about what he called "your latest separation." I hadn't the strength to argue with him. When I hung up, my hand was trembling as usual. After that, I tried a couple of her old flatmates, some colleagues from work, even a couple in a converted vicarage in Northumberland with whom she often spent painting weekends. Nothing. Absolutely nothing. I was growing scared.

I rang London again around eight o'clock. This time Tim came to the phone.

"Peter," he said, "why aren't you being straight with me? Something must have made her leave."

"We were getting along fine," I answered. "It's just that . . ." I told him what I could.

"That doesn't sound like Sarah," was all he said.

"None of this is like Sarah," I retorted.

"I think you should go to the police."

"What, and have them poking their noses into everything? They'd get nowhere."

"You're getting nowhere yourself. And unlike you, they know the district. You should have gone to them before this. How long has it been?"

"Nearly forty-eight hours."

"Jesus, Peter—that's far too long. Get in touch with them tonight. Drive over."

"I can't. I can't leave the house. In case she comes back."

"Well, ring them then."

I didn't, not right away, not that night. That night something happened—something that unsettled me for a long time afterward. I had spent the evening trying to write, but it had been useless. My mind was not on the story but on Sarah. I kept listening, half expecting to hear her feet outside the door, or her voice calling from the kitchen. Intermittently I would look up, as though the telephone was about to ring, thinking she had at last decided to call a halt and make her reappearance. But there was nothing all evening.

The devil of it was that I loved her very much. We had been married thirteen years. I had come close to destroying our life together, I know, and Sarah had taken a long time to forgive me. Nonetheless, I loved her, and her absence distressed me terribly. I could not bear the thought of separation, of real, lasting separation, of never seeing her again. And that other, darker thought, the possibility that something unpleasant had happened to her, that filled me with dread.

Around midnight, depressed by my fruitless vigil, I

trudged upstairs. I was in no mood for sleep, yet the thought of spending the rest of the night downstairs was loathsome. At the entrance to our bedroom, I hesitated. The thought had caught me unawares, that I should look at the paintings Sarah had completed, the ones she had stored on the top floor. She had been working that day, the day she had disappeared; irrationally, I thought I might find some sort of clue in the painting she had last completed.

In spite of my newfound curiosity, I was strangely reluctant to go farther up the stairs. My dream had affected me. There was a melancholy feel to the entire upper story of the house, and I still felt a little spooked by the bedroom I had been in, the one in which I had sensed that atmosphere of subdued yet growing menace. I went up all the same. I knew that if I let my fears get the better of me, I would soon end up like Sarah, frightened out of my wits and forced to leave. I had no intentions of leaving, not until my two months were up.

The room in which the finished paintings had been left was at the end of a short corridor, just beyond the bedroom, now locked and silent. I switched on the light and looked around. No furniture, just a large rectangle covered in a white sheet, propped against one wall.

There was a portfolio under the sheet. I laid it flat on the bare floor and untied the ribbons one by one. Carefully, I opened it. Inside was a stack of heavy papers, each sheet laid neatly on the one below.

I had expected paintings of the house and gardens, or of the coastal views visible from the cliff top. But the painting on top was not a landscape at all. It was a portrait of a woman sitting in a room. With a shudder, I thought I recognized the room—it was the one farther down the corridor, the one that Sarah had considered the heart of whatever ailed this house.

The woman in the painting sat tensely on a high-backed chair, her body upright, I would almost have said stiff. She wore a long black dress with buttons that went from a high neck to her ankles, and her hair was lifted and arranged in a tight bun on top. Her age I guessed to be somewhere between eighty and ninety. Sarah had painted her face well, and in considerable detail. One side of the face was completely in shadow. On it was a look I could not quite interpret. Unease, perhaps, or the memory of something unpleasant. Or the first stirrings of dread.

I lifted the painting and set it to one side. Beneath it was a second, almost identical. The same room, the same time of day, the same woman on the chair. What on earth had been going through Sarah's mind all the time she had been out there in the garden, painting? I drew the second picture aside as well. The one beneath was the same.

No, not quite. It was at the third painting that I noticed a tiny but marked difference between the three pictures I had seen so far. On the wall behind the sitter was the damp patch I had noticed in the room. In each of the pictures, the shape of the patch changed slightly, and it seemed to be growing in several directions.

Quickly, I leafed through the remaining pictures. There were nine in all. They all showed the same scene. In the last, the damp patch had grown until it covered most of the wall. And I could see, when I looked more closely, that the wallpaper was about to give in one place. I bent down and brought the light right up to the picture. As I did so I shuddered. In the painting, against the wallpaper, pressing hard as though about to burst through, was the unmistakable shape of a child's hand.

CHAPTER 7

I RANG THE POLICE early the next morning. The night I passed was difficult. There were bad dreams. Or, rather, the same dream as before. And when I woke, bad thoughts. There were noises somewhere in the house, but I did not investigate them. I knew Sarah had not made them, and I did not want to know who had.

The policeman who took my call suggested that I ought to call at the station in order to file a missing-person report. After checking with Tim and Susan that Sarah had still not turned up in London, I drove to St. Ives. The main police station was in Will's Lane, next to Trewyn Gardens. A desk sergeant showed me to a side room. About ten minutes later a young police-woman came to take details of Sarah's disappearance. I had brought a photograph, one of the shots we had taken at St. Just's church. It had been developed at the pharmacy in Tredannack. They noted it and filed it away, together with a detailed description and an account of my efforts until then.

"It's well over forty-eight hours," the policewoman said. Her voice was neutral, there was no hint of accusation in it that I can remember. That was what I feared, of course: accusation, the leveling of guilt, the implication that I had done something to Sarah and that my innocence was mere posturing.

At this time of year my limbs ache. I am sometimes afraid without reason of small things, of shadows, of movements spied from the eye's corner.

"I'm sorry?" I said.

"Why did you take so long before notifying us?"

"It's not so long," I said. "I had every reason to think she'd turn up by now. Why not? She's not a child. It isn't as if she was in obvious danger."

"But you say she took no money, no spare clothes. By the next day that must have been a great inconvenience for her."

"I don't know. She may have had money. She has her own bank account. I don't know how much she had in her handbag to start with."

"I think she'd have taken the bag. Most women would. Did she have credit cards?"

I nodded.

"And are they still in the bag?"

"Yes."

"All of them?"

"Yes, I think so. I'd have to check. There's Visa, Access, one or two shop cards."

"Normally we wouldn't investigate an adult disappearance at this stage," she said slowly, watching me, as though expecting some reaction. "People often walk out on their spouses. If your wife wants to be on her own, that's her business. You do understand that, don't you?"

"She hasn't walked out," I insisted. "She would have taken her things."

"Yes, I understand that, sir. That's why I think we may have to take a closer look. I'll get in touch with headquarters at Camborne. If the super agrees, he'll send someone out this afternoon to take a look around. They'll want to see if there's anything you've missed."

I looked at her, not knowing what to say or do. My name had meant nothing to her. I was a stranger. Just a man whose wife had walked away into darkness.

Small movements in the half shadows frighten me, and the voices of small children.

Two constables came and searched the house. One of them took a walk through the grounds. Birds were singing.

"Did you have a fight?" his colleague asked, back in the house, in the library. I had been writing, and papers were strewn across the table.

"No," I said. "Not a fight."

I tried to explain, to make him understand.

"The house, you say? She was afraid of it?"

"Yes. It's an old house. It has memories. She thought something had happened here, something unpleasant."

"This woman, the one in the pub. What did you say her name was?"

"Trebarvah. Margaret Trebarvah. But you can ask any of the locals. They all know about the house."

He jotted down the name in his notebook.

"I daresay. But it's your wife I'm interested in at present."

He was young, with a fair mustache. For all his pleasant manner, I could see the seeds of suspicion.

Perhaps, he was thinking, I am sure of it, perhaps the terrible thing had happened more recently. Perhaps I had done away with Sarah and was now attempting to put the police off my track. I am sure that was what was going through his mind. Or something very like it.

The constable shivered.

"It's cold in here," he said.

I said nothing.

On damp days my bones swell. I can smell the sea, even if I am far inland. And with the smell come other things, unbidden. The sound of the sea is merciless and repetitive. And there are other sounds I fear. I pretend I do not hear them, but they are there.

That evening I went to Tredannack, to the Green Dragon. Ted was there behind the bar as usual, and Doreen, his wife, in a green dress. He served me a pint of Old Cornish. As I lifted it he asked after Sarah.

"Isn't your wife with you tonight, Mr. Clare?"

I thought of lying, but I had no strength for subterfuge.

"She's missing," I said. "She hasn't been to Tredannack by any chance, has she?"

He shook his head, looking at me oddly.

"I've not seen her myself. What do you mean 'missing'?"

I explained as best I could.

"It was the house," I said. "It chased her away."

"I reckon so."

"Tell me, is Margaret Trebarvah here tonight?"

He shook his head.

"She may be in later," he said. "Depends what's on the telly. Margaret's a great one for that."

"I'd like to speak to her. Let me know if she comes in."

He nodded, and turned to serve his next customer. I was ignored as usual. By force of habit, I took my glass to a corner table. A few eyes followed me.

It was near closing time when I looked up and saw Ted Bickleigh standing next to me.

"Margaret Trebarvah's just come in," he said. "Doreen's serving her now. She sometimes has a pint before bedtime. I reckon it's her excuse to keep out of the way till Bill's fast asleep. If you catch my meaning. She's never been the same since the kiddie disappeared."

"The kiddie?"

"Didn't you know? They had a little girl. Three or four, she was. It happened about five years ago. Went out to play one day and never come back. Police looked everywhere, but they never found a body. Reckon one'll turn up in time, though. They always do."

Had that been what drew Sarah to Margaret Trebarvah? I wondered. Would Sarah "turn up" one day, a small, sad corpse in someone's woodland?

Margaret Trebarvah was a small, ruined woman in her midthirties. She had never been pretty, never been happy. Her eyes were watery and furtive. Whenever I tried to hold them, they would shift away, now to this corner, now to that. She sat before me, arms crossed defensively, mouth set, as though pinned to her seat. I could tell that her husband beat her. Where it would not show. His grief for the child would have been turned on her.

"Would you like a drink, Margaret?" I asked.

"Got a drink," she muttered, looking away.

"Let me get you another one. There's still a bit before Ted calls time. What would you like?"

"Got all I want."

"All right, then. Do you mind if I sit down? I'd like a word with you."

She shifted, as though thinking of standing up and leaving. I noticed we were being watched.

"I saw you here three nights ago," I said. "My wife said you'd had a little chat, you and her. It upset her, but she wouldn't tell me what it was about. I thought maybe you'd tell me. Seeing as it concerns me."

She looked up from her drink—a pint of bitter— then let her eyes slide away.

"She'll tell herself if you ask," she mumbled. "No reason not to."

"I can't ask her. She's gone. Vanished."

That got her attention. There was no mistaking the look of sheer terror that crossed her face. Then, drawing herself in—as she was no doubt well accustomed to doing when Bill lashed out—she took a mouthful from her glass.

"Gone back to London, has she?"

"I don't know. I was hoping you might give me a clue. You told her something about our house. You frightened her. Later that night she got out of bed and walked off. Why? What was she thinking of? I think you know. Or can guess."

She looked up, raising her head very slowly. People were still stealing glances. It would soon be closing time.

"What makes you think she's gone?"

"What?"

"Maybe she hasn't gone. Maybe she's still there. Have you thought of that? Have you?"

"What happened there? Why won't you tell me?"

She gave me a wretched look, like someone who feels sick.

"And have it happen over again? We've enough

troubles, mister, without the likes of you coming here and stirring up what you don't understand."

She drained her glass. Her eyes were full of some sort of pain. She stood.

"Margaret, please. What happened? I have to know."

She leaned across the table.

"There was a woman," she said. "A young woman. This was in the days before the road. There was just a lane then, mud and that. She lived in Petherick House with her father. He'd a black temper, a man's temper. Got her pregnant, so they say. Or maybe not, maybe there was another man, I don't know. But he'd never let her out after that. Something was done to the baby; they say she killed it. God knows. But he kept her locked up in one room for a year or more after. And then she died. Of a broken heart, they say. Or he killed her."

She stopped. She had come to the end of her story.

"That's all there is?"

"She's there still. She won't let go, doesn't know how to. Trapped."

"What age? What age of woman was she?"

"Don't know. This is all handed down, I've never seen a photograph or nothing. She was young, they say. Twenty-five or so."

She got to her feet. Heads turned.

"What else?" I asked. I knew there was more. But she went out without answering.

On returning, I went up to the bedroom. I had been stupid, I had not checked the most obvious thing, because it had not occurred to me to do so. If Sarah had gotten out of bed and gone out, she must have changed into outdoor wear of some kind. But when I looked through the room again, I could not think of anything that was missing. Except for one thing: her nightgown.

In my dream that night, I climbed to the first landing. It was dark, very dark. When I woke, the house all around me was still. But I felt sure, I do not know why, I felt sure that if I had wakened just moments earlier, I would have heard something.

CHAPTER 8

THE NEXT DAY I was visited by the detective chief inspector from Camborne Division, a man called Raleigh. With him was an assistant, a much younger man whose name I forgot then and have never since remembered. Raleigh held all my attention during that visit. He was a coarse man, ill-bred and ill-mannered, yet he was astonishingly aware of these and other deficiencies, and I sensed how powerful an effort he exerted at all times to correct himself, to modify by a word here or a gesture there the impression of boorishness or rudeness he knew he must be making. Later, on examining his behavior and going back over his questions in my mind, I realized that he was, in fact, a highly intelligent man, a man who had come far by much effort, but who would, he knew, go no further in life. His manner held him back, his primitiveness, the curse of roughness that his parents had so unwittingly laid upon him at birth.

"Is your name Clare?"

"Peter Clare, yes." I was standing in the doorway, dressed in an open-necked shirt and light trousers. I had been in the garden at the back when the car drew up.

"I'd like to have a word with you."

He was standing on the doorstep with the air of a man who will not be sent away.

"Well, I . . . I don't know. Who exactly . . . ?"

He handed me a card. Half a dozen steps behind him, his colleague lurked, embarrassed or just diffident.

"Well, Chief Inspector," I went on, handing the card back to him. "I don't really know. I've given all the details I know to the policewoman who interviewed me in St. Ives. I wasn't planning—"

"I don't have all day, you know. Are you going to leave us standing here or what?"

I could see there was no getting rid of him. I could hardly have shut the door in his face.

"You'd better come on in, then."

He turned and spoke gruffly to the younger man. "Don't stand there gawping."

I took them to the drawing room.

"Can I get you anything? Tea? Coffee?"

"Don't drink either. Sit down. I'd like to get this over with."

He had already taken a chair and was pointing me toward one facing it. His assistant shifted for himself, bringing a hard chair from the back of the room and setting it near us. I noticed him take a tape recorder from his pocket.

"Is that necessary?" I asked. "It's not as if—"

"Saves time. You can have it off if you like. But I'd prefer it on." He hesitated. "If you don't mind."

"Very well, if you like. I take it you've come to talk about Sarah."

"Sarah, yes. Your wife."

The underling switched the machine on and placed it gently on the table beside me. I wondered if it would pick up the low growl of the sea outside.

"Your parents-in-law have been in touch with their local police, Mr. Clare. They're worried about your wife, what's become of her. They don't seem to have much faith in your efforts to find her. I'd call that interfering, but it's not my place to say. What about you? Do you reckon that's a fair line for them to take?"

The information startled me into denial.

"No. No, I don't. It is interference, you're quite right. I don't see what the hell they can be thinking about, poking their noses in like this. I've done what I can. I've been frantic, worried sick. They're not even here, they don't know what's been going on."

But they did not need to, I thought. I did not doubt that they could come up with all sorts of possibilities, enough possibilities to prompt a detective chief inspector to come down here to see for himself.

"And what exactly has been going on, Mr. Clare?"

He took a cigarette from a packet of Benson and Hedges and lit it. He neither asked permission nor offered one to me. I dislike cigarette smoke. I was asthmatic as a child. Smoke still provokes a cough in me. From time to time I use an inhaler. And in the nights, in winter, my breathing is sometimes uneven. In the nights. In winter.

"You know what's been going on. I gave a statement in St. Ives."

"I know, but I'd like it from you. Horse's mouth, as it were. In your own words. You're a writer, I believe. I don't read much myself. Don't have the time. But I expect you've got a way with words."

I related yet again the events of the past few days.

Without drama, in what I believed were flat and neutral tones, or the nearest to those that I could approximate.

Raleigh listened attentively, sucking absently yet quite fiercely on his cigarette. When it came to an end, he lit a second cigarette from the butt before crushing it between his fingers and putting it in his pocket.

I finished my account. Raleigh sat for a while without speaking, smoking his cigarette, watching me.

"Mr. Clare," he said finally, "exactly what do you take me for?"

"I'm sorry?"

"Your story doesn't even begin to hang together. You now say your wife went out in her night attire—"

It was a curious phrase for him to use. Archaic.

"Probably."

"—without any money that you're aware of. And all because some woman in the pub takes it into her head to spin a yarn about a haunted house. They're two-a-penny 'round here, haunted houses. Then it takes you over two days to report your good lady missing."

"Well, I'm sorry, but that is what happened."

"You'll excuse me if I say I don't frigging believe you. Pardon my French."

He dropped the half-smoked cigarette onto the carpet and stubbed it out with his heel.

"Well, thank you, Mr. Clare," he said, standing. "I can't say but that I'm disappointed, what with you being a writer and all. I'd thought you writers were clever at telling tales. Or is that it? You think a tale that makes no sense, something nobody would think for a moment could be convincing, that a tale like that might take me in? What is it the French call that? *Faux naïf*? You're a sight too complicated for the likes of me, Mr. Clare. Still, I daresay you'll tell me the truth when you've a mind to.

"In the meantime, I'll have them send over some dogs from Penzance. They're good dogs, they've got good noses. They could smell a fart behind glass in a force-ten gale, if you'll excuse the expression. We'll see if they can't pick up your wife's trail. The sergeant here will hang on till they come. Maybe he'll have that cup of tea you were telling me about earlier. He drinks Earl Grey, if you have any. If not, Lapsang will do nicely."

He glanced down at the carpet.

"Sorry about the mess," he said. "Filthy habit."

But he did not bend to pick up the butt.

As he made to go he glanced down at the table. A copy of *The Times* was lying open at the crossword. I had completed most of it, but got stuck at 7 across, a word of ten letters with an apparently straightforward clue: *Room can supply wine.*

"Chambertin," he said, and left.

Why hadn't I thought of that?

The dogs found nothing. I gave them items from Sarah's wardrobe, and they picked up trails everywhere, all of them leading to her usual places inside the house or in the gardens. But there was no trail that led very far, and none at all on the path to the main gate: we had always gone that way by car, never on foot. Had a car come for her after all that night, unnoticed by me?

When they had finished, Raleigh returned, a cigarette in his mouth.

"Seems your wife didn't leave Petherick House after all, Mr. Clare," he said. "Leastwise, not on foot."

"But she had to," I insisted. "I would have seen a car. Or heard it. She didn't fly out."

"She might have swum," he said, glancing away toward the cliff. "We'll keep looking."

There were men in the woods, fanning out and

thrashing their way through the undergrowth, a long file of them, and two dogs. They took all that afternoon and the best part of the evening. Shortly before dark, they came back empty-handed.

"This is absurd," I said for the hundredth time that day. "She's in London by now, or somewhere else. But not here. You're wasting your time. Your bloody dogs are mistaken."

"They're good dogs, Mr. Clare. The best. I'd not say a word against them dogs, not if I was you."

"What now?" I asked.

"I'd like to search the house, Mr. Clare. If you've no objection."

"The house? What on earth for?"

He shook his head.

"I don't know, to tell you the truth. But I'd like a proper look-round. While we're here."

"There's nothing," I said. "Sarah isn't here."

"Yes, I know that, Mr. Clare. But it's best to look at everything. You'll admit that's best, won't you?"

I let them look. They went through everything, into every room, but it did not take long. I thought they were going to leave empty-handed, but at the last moment Raleigh came down the stairs. There was something in his hand.

"Can you tell me how this got upstairs?" he asked.

It was Sarah's hat, or what was left of it. I must have left it in the room on the top floor where I had found it. Raleigh held it in both hands now.

"I don't know," I stumbled. "It . . . it was there on Monday night. Torn up, just like that. Sarah must have put it there herself."

"Mr. Clare, I'd like you to come to the station with me. You don't have to, not at the moment, but I'm worried about some things, and it would be a help to me if you came. We could clear some things up."

*   *   *

I went with him reluctantly. He did not say so, but I knew he suspected me of something, of doing away with Sarah perhaps. Possibly my in-laws had told him things, voicing old feelings, slandering me. I answered his questions as best I could. He had nothing to hold me on, of course: just a shredded hat and some inconsistencies in my story. The questioning went on until well after midnight, sometimes gentle, sometimes harsh, but it got us nowhere. We were both exhausted by then. He told me I could go home. But as I made for the door it opened and his assistant came in, the one whose name I cannot remember.

He looked nervous. In one hand he was holding something. A tape.

"I'd like you to hear this, sir," he said. "You, too, Mr. Clare," he went on, looking at me.

I sat down again. We were in an interview room, pale green walls and a smell of old sweat. A plain table held the center space. The nameless policeman put his tape into the machine on the tabletop.

"This is the recording I made earlier today," he said. "Your interview with Mr. Clare at Petherick House. I'd just started transcribing it."

He switched the machine on.

Hissing, then the sound of Raleigh's voice.

Your parents-in-law have been in touch with their local police, Mr. Clare . . .

Then my voice, replying.

No. No, I don't. It is interference, you're quite right . . .

And what exactly has been going on, Mr. Clare?

At first, all seemed as I remember it. The interview proceeded, answer following question, question answer, all as it had done earlier that day. I could not understand what it could be that the policeman wanted us to hear. No one said anything. The policeman sat there, his eyes fixed on the recorder, his face tense. The tape turned, hissing. Now my voice, now Raleigh's. Then, barely perceptible at first, another sound began to make itself felt.

We could hear it in the background at first, like a sound very far away. I glanced at Raleigh. His face betrayed puzzlement at first, then settled into disbelief. He looked at me, as though I had the answer. I did not move. Suddenly I was very cold. A sense of horror was crawling across my skin. We listened together, and the voices continued: my voice, Raleigh's voice, and now, quite unmistakable, something else, something none of us had heard that afternoon. The sound of a small child crying loudly, its thin voice rising and falling, but growing all the time in volume until, suddenly, it drowned us out completely.

CHAPTER 9

ALL I REMEMBER about that moment is the horror and how it took steady hold of us. Things are different now, of course. I have seen and heard more than babies crying. I know who the child was. And I know why she cried. Why she cries. But the horror remains.

Raleigh and his assistant came to the house again the next day. With them were other policemen with sophisticated recording equipment sent down early that morning from Truro; but they got nothing. Not a whisper. To this day it remains a mystery why the child's crying should have been audible on that first tape and not on any subsequent recording. And it is as much a mystery how it came to be there at all, when none of us had heard a thing that day other than our own voices. The tape had been brand new, and expert opinion agreed that there was no way in which the recording of one voice could have been superimposed on that of another, using that equipment. And yet it was there, unremovable, fixed, like a dull stain that will not be wiped out.

Raleigh's behavior toward me changed from that moment. I think he half believed what I had told him about the house being haunted.

Have I told you I sleep with the light on? Every night, summer and winter, it makes no difference. Some nights I do not sleep at all.

I want to show you something. It will only take a moment. Look, here's my room, the room I sleep or lie awake in every night. That's a photograph of Sarah on the bedside table, that's the pen I use when I write in bed, that's a book of essays I'm reading at the moment, those are the analgesics I use to deaden the pain when my back hurts, that I will use for a more serious purpose one day soon. Very soon. It's a quiet room without mirrors. Take your time. But listen— can you hear anything? If you stay the night, you'll hear more. Much more.

But no one ever stays the night.

In the end, the police reached the conclusion that Sarah had fallen—or been pushed to her death—from the cliff. It would have been high tide, around 2:00 A.M. Her body would be washed ashore in due course, and that would be that.

For my part, I thought it unlikely. I knew she would not have jumped, I did not think she would have been careless enough to stray there in the darkness, and I knew I had not pushed her. Since her disappearance, I had heard enough—though not, as yet, seen anything—in the house to convince me that something had happened there for which I could find no rational explanation, for which no rational explanation might exist. The house held a secret of some sort, and I grew more and more convinced that if only I could solve it, I might also solve the riddle of Sarah's disappearance.

During the days Raleigh and his men were in or near the house, nothing happened there. It grew very still. But I sensed that whatever lay buried there was merely biding its time, that there was more, much more, to come.

One thing did not stop: the dreams. Every night I started out on my slow climb up the stairs, and every night when I woke, I had gone a little higher. That was all that ever varied. The darkness, the silence, the brooding expectancy, the sense of malice somewhere in the house—all those remained as they had been before. And each night I woke sweating, barking like a dog without a kennel.

I stayed. What else was there to do? In a sense, where else could I have gone? I stayed and waited, though I did not know for what. I started writing again, a little at first, then vast quantities. It was my only distraction. Nothing else helped me forget, though there were times when I sat, almost thoughtless, in the study or outdoors in the garden watching the birds turn. Each day there were phone calls to make: between me and the police, between me and Sue, between me and Sarah's parents. I know no form of waiting worse than that. The anxiety is not relieved by the passage of time. Every avenue of inquiry ended in a wall. A wall in which there was no sign of any door. Or, if I am totally honest, in which the only door was a familiar one that led into an empty room on top of the house.

*　　*　　*

The second month ended. I spent as little time in the house as possible. During the days, I stayed in the garden, writing. Or I took the car and drove through the countryside for miles, without really going anywhere. Every so often, a view or a smell would awaken a memory from childhood. And then the pain of the present would overlay the memory and turn it into something else. I cannot listen to the sea now, or smell magnolia, or hear sea gulls cry without remembering that summer.

My lease at Petherick House was due to run out. Medawar, my contact at the solicitors, would not hear of an extension. I started to pack for the journey back to London. The most difficult thing was putting Sarah's clothes away in their case. She had not seemed completely gone until that moment. I took each item in turn from the wardrobe, folded it, and laid it in the suitcase, knowing they might never be taken out again.

As I folded her blue linen jacket I felt something hard in the pocket. It was a small diary, a pocket-size organizer with a leather binding for which she bought refills every year. I flicked through it casually. The last significant entry had been for the date of our departure. The rest of the pages were blank. Except for one, the twelfth of July, four days before her disappearance. In the tiny space for that day, Sarah had made an entry, just a name and a telephone number: *Miss Trevorrow: 97 Lemon Street, Truro.*

The next day I showed the entry to Raleigh. He agreed that it might be worthwhile to check on this Miss Trevorrow and suggested we visit her together. We went early the next morning, the day before I was due to leave. The assistant drove. His name still does not come back to me. We took the A30 as far as Blackwater, where we branched off for the city. The A30 was packed with cars and caravans, long lines of tourists heading home. And for every one that left, it seemed that two were heading down on the other side. The fine weather had not abated.

We arrived just after 10:00. It was an old house in what had once been the fashionable center of the city. The wide street in which it stood had been solidly residential, but now shops and offices had taken over. Though never grand, the house had in its day been well proportioned, but over the years it had lost its loveliness. It was badly in need of repointing and repainting. There were slates missing from the roof, and the front door did not hang quite straight. I thought it a sad, abandoned place. But someone lived there. Even the most neglected house is somebody's home.

The door was opened by a middle-aged woman who resembled the house. Like it, she was tired and faded and in need of a few coats of paint. Lank hair fell on rounded shoulders. She wore a blouse that had not been washed in at least a week.

"Miss Trevorrow?" Raleigh asked.

She looked at him blankly, as though deaf or half-witted.

"My name's Raleigh," he said. "Chief Inspector Raleigh." He held out a card. Her eye fell on it without interest. "May we come in?" he went on, all politeness, though I think he knew it was wasted. We hung back, the nameless subordinate and I.

"My name's not Trevorrow," the woman said. A voice without energy. "There's no one by that name here."

"This is ninety-seven Lemon Street, isn't it?"

She seemed to hesitate, then nodded.

"Well, then, Miss Trevorrow, I wonder if you'd mind letting us in. I need to ask a few questions. About a Mrs. Clare."

She looked blankly at us.

"Clare? Don't know nobody called Clare. And I already told you, my name's not Trevorrow. It's Rudd. Evelyn Rudd. Mrs., not miss. I'll get my husband, if you like."

Before Raleigh could stop her, she called back down the dingy hallway. Moments later a dull-eyed, potbellied man appeared. He had the slackness of the unemployed or the newly retired. No purpose, no reason for being where he was.

"What is it, Evie? What's going on at our door?"

"It's the police, Bill," she whined. "The police here, asking questions."

"At our house? Questions at our house?"

Raleigh did his best to explain. Bill Rudd was as uncomprehending as his wife, as little interested in the small drama on his doorstep. He glanced away from time to time, catching my eye and losing it as quickly. I was watching his wife, her little movements as she looked on from the dim safety of the hall, where it smelled of something sour.

"May we come in, at least?" Raleigh insisted. "I need to ask a few questions. About a Mrs. Clare."

They both looked blankly at us.

"Clare?" said Mr. Rudd. "Don't know nobody called Clare."

"All the same. I do have to speak with you."

There was no help for it. The Rudds let us pass. Evelyn showed us into what she called the front parlor, a wretched place of faded antimacassars and cheap china stashed behind glass. I had not thought people possessed front parlors anymore. An old telephone with a dial sat on a low, fringed stool.

We all sat uneasily. Raleigh took Sarah's diary from his pocket and showed it to the Rudds in turn.

"That is your address, isn't it?"

They said nothing, as though hoping that a long enough silence would drive him away.

"Well?" asked Raleigh. "You must know something about this Trevorrow woman. Is she a friend of yours? A lodger? Relative?"

"Got no friends," muttered Bill. I was not surprised.

"Perhaps you'd both like to come down to the station with me," Raleigh said. "You might find it easier to answer my questions there."

They glowered at him, but said nothing.

Without asking permission, Raleigh picked up the phone and made to dial. Then, with a gesture of disgust, he slammed the receiver down again.

"Dead as a fucking dodo," he exclaimed.

"Language!" admonished Evelyn, animated for the first time since our arrival. "I won't allow language in this house."

"No language," repeated her husband, nodding doglike. "Not in here."

"Does anyone other than yourselves have access to this house?" Raleigh asked, disregarding the scolding. "Your daughter perhaps? She wouldn't be called Trevorrow, by any chance?"

"No daughter," Bill Rudd snapped. "Don't have a daughter, we. Never have had. No children. Of either kind."

I noticed that he did not say "sex." No doubt that, too, would have constituted "language." No language, no children, probably no sex. And, it would seem, no Miss Trevorrow.

"No one who comes in?"

"Who would?" Mrs. Rudd asked. "Who would come in?" It was not a necessary question, and Raleigh knew it. Still, he had his duty to do, his own questions to ask. He went on asking them, but I could see he had no heart for the task, not any longer. In the end, he gave up. Telling the Rudds he would still want them for a formal interview, he stormed out.

We drove back to Penzance, puzzled and dejected. There was still no news of Sarah. I knew there was never going to be news. Wherever she had gone, she was not on any road that the police or I could follow her down.

The house was quiet. As always, I filled the electric meter with coins. I had to be sure of light. Even while I slept I kept the hall and landings illuminated. I had one last night to spend.

Raleigh rang about five that afternoon. Bill Rudd had been in touch.

"He rang a few minutes ago, Mr. Clare. From a phone box. I thought you'd like to know what he told me—though I can't see what help it is to us."

He sounded more distant than he had been.

"What did he say?"

"He remembered a Miss Trevorrow after all," Raleigh said—reluctantly, I thought. "Agnes Trevorrow. Seems she used to live in the house. In fact, she was the previous owner. She'd been there a long time, apparently; Rudd didn't know how long."

"When was this?"

"When?" He paused. "About forty years ago. The Rudds bought the house in 1953, the year of the coronation. It's about the only thing Rudd seems to remember."

"They bought it from this Miss Trevorrow?"

There was a short silence on the line. I could hear the faint sound of Raleigh's breathing. His voice when it returned was tense.

"No," he said. "From her solicitor. Miss Trevorrow was dead."

CHAPTER

10

RALEIGH DID NOT want me to leave, not right away. The next morning I moved into a hotel near Penzance, in a small place on the coast, Marazion. My room had a view of St. Michael's Mount, and of the sea beyond. This was the southern side of the peninsula. I had my back to Petherick House and that other water, the water in which Raleigh thought my wife had drowned.

His sympathy for me seemed to have drained away. He simply could no longer believe my story.

"Why would I lie?" I asked. "There'd be no point. You'd be bound to see through it before long. I'm not a stupid man, you know that."

"Well, that's just it, isn't it? I know you're not stupid. That's why I think there has to be something else behind what I'd take for stupidity in anyone else."

"The entry was in Sarah's hand," I said. "You can have one of your experts check that out."

"They've already done so," he answered.

I spent the first day sitting at my window, trying to write. The mood would not come here, in spite of the beauty of that view. Or, perhaps, because of it.

Early one morning, Raleigh called. His faithful sidekick was with him as usual. What earthly use he was to the chief inspector, I could never tell.

"I'd like you to come with us, Mr. Clare," Raleigh said. "Another trip. I'd like you to have a word with the solicitors who rented the house to you."

"They won't know anything," I said.

"They'll know who owns the place."

We drove on a day of squalls to St. Ives. Raleigh talked about himself for the first time. He told me about his wife, who had divorced him five years earlier, messily, it seemed. He had two children, both at university, one studying philosophy, the other Sanskrit —matters of which he knew nothing and wished to know nothing. He was a sad man, I thought, someone for whom life had not worked out quite as it had promised. It seemed to me that it must be worse for policemen, as it is for doctors. They see our failures at first hand. The worst side of human nature every day. No doubt policemen think us all criminals in time. It's just a matter of what is known and what is hidden.

The firm of solicitors was a long-established one, with offices above a shop in St. Ives—Pentreath, Single, and Nesbitt were the names on the plate. I asked for Medawar, but we were shown instead into the office of Mr. Pentreath.

"Well, gentlemen," he said, rising from his desk. "What can I do for you?"

He was a dark-faced man, ebullient yet restrained.

He would be the partner who dealt with wills and mortgages, and other domestic matters, a man capable of putting at ease clients unfamiliar with the intricacies of the law. Not jolly, that would have been out of place; but never fully serious. He had something beneath his surface, a sense of humor or something more bizarre, perhaps. I put him at fifty, though I have no doubt he'll look just the same in another ten or twenty years.

The preliminaries done with, Raleigh explained the purpose of our visit. When he came to a close, it was evident that something was troubling Pentreath. The solicitor turned to me.

"You have papers confirming your rental of the property in question?"

I showed him the letters I had had from Medawar. He looked through them slowly and passed them back without a word. I could see he was worried about something.

"If you'll excuse me for a moment," he said, rising, "there's something I have to check."

He stayed away for ten minutes or more. We did not talk during his absence. Solicitors' offices are not furnished for chitchat. Pentreath's shelves were stacked with the conventional apparatus of the small-town legal expert: row after row of legal texts in stiff bindings, some with their spines ruffed and broken. There was a small window. Through it I watched the sky and white birds in it circling.

Pentreath returned looking more anxious than ever. Another man accompanied him, whom he introduced to us as Mr. Nesbitt. Nesbitt was elderly and thin, with a high dome of pure white hair. His fingers were stained with nicotine, and his clothes gave off a smell of tobacco smoke. He sat down facing me.

"Mr. Clare," he said, "I regret to say that you have

been the victim of a most unfortunate fraud. The young man with whom you had dealings, Ian Medawar, was dismissed from the firm two weeks ago. He had been caught falsifying expenses. But now it seems as if he was up to rather more than that. The fact is that he had no authority to rent Petherick House to you. The house belongs to a client in the north of England, a Mr. Adderstone. In all the years we have been handling the house for him, Mr. Adderstone has repeatedly given strict instructions that it must under no circumstances be let out. He has always been most insistent on that point.

"It now seems that Mr. Medawar chose to ignore those instructions in order to take the rent for himself. Obviously, we shall have to place the matter in the hands of the police. In the meantime, we will be more than happy to repay you in full. Should any question of compensation arise—"

He stopped, visibly unhappy at the thought of legal action, glancing from Raleigh to myself as if trying to determine which of us represented the greater threat. I reassured him that I had not come in search of compensation. I had, after all, received what I had paid for.

Still apologizing profusely, Nesbitt stood and made for the door. He stood outside for a moment, his back visible through the frosted glass. I heard the sound of a matchbox being opened, then the scrape as he struck a light.

"We really are sorry about this," said Pentreath, resuming his seat. "If anything has happened as a result of this swindle . . . What is it exactly that you came for?"

"We want to know about Petherick House," said Raleigh. "Ownership, past and present. Inheritances, purchases—whatever you can tell us."

The solicitor went to a filing cabinet at the rear of the room and from it took an armful of files of assorted sizes, all tied with pink ribbon. Papers spilled from some. The computer and its mixed blessings had not reached Pentreath, Single, and Nesbitt. I wondered to myself what manner of man was Single.

"Most of these old files should have been sent to storage long ago," said Pentreath, dropping the heap onto his desk. "Now, if you will give me a few more minutes in which to remind myself of the facts."

He scanned the top layer of files, taking each one in his hands and bringing its contents close to his face: he was evidently shortsighted. He grunted and nodded amiably as he did so, glancing up from time to time at Raleigh or myself in order to flash a reassuring smile. It was a look of feigned complicity, as though to say he shared in our dismay at such a mass of paperwork. The nameless subordinate he ignored.

"Well," he said at last, sinking back in his seat, "all seems to be in order. Where would you like me to begin?"

"You can start by telling me more about this Mr. Adderstone."

"Yes, of course. As Mr. Nesbitt explained, he is the current owner of Petherick House. His full name is Richard Adderstone. From time to time we transact business on his behalf down here. Mr. Adderstone lives in Yorkshire and visits Cornwall only rarely. It is such a long journey, and he is getting on in years. But he is a Cornishman by birth, and I believe he lived in these parts until he was thirty or thereabouts. Petherick House has remained empty since then. We look after it for him. See that it's kept in a reasonable state of repair and so on. Mr. Clare here is the first person to have stayed in the property in all this time."

He paused and opened a slim file.

"I believe the house was left to Mr. Adderstone by a great aunt who died in—let me see . . ."

Pentreath leafed through a thick pile of yellowing papers in the file, then pulled out what he had been looking for.

"Nineteen fifty-three. July 1953."

Raleigh looked at me. I did not move a muscle. "What was her name?" Raleigh asked. I could feel the tension in his voice.

"Trevorrow," Pentreath said. "Miss Agnes Trevorrow."

Raleigh looked at me again. He showed no sign of surprise. A deep silence followed. I shivered in spite of myself. Pentreath looked at each of us in turn, puzzled by our reaction.

When he spoke again, Raleigh's voice was measured, as though he feared what an unguarded question might uncover.

"And this Miss Trevorrow lived at Petherick House right up to the time of her death?"

Pentreath shook his head.

"Not entirely," he said. "She had lived there for a very long time. I understand she was quite elderly when she passed away. We still have a copy of her will to hand, and other papers relating to the house. But she also owned a smaller property in Truro. I believe she went there to live from time to time, but in the end she always went back to Petherick House. She died there, and she was buried in the churchyard at Tredannack. The house in Truro was sold by us and the proceeds put into her estate. Since Mr. Adderstone was by then her only surviving relative, her will left everything to him. The sale of the Truro property was carried out on his instructions. But there was an entail which prevented—and still prevents—him from putting Petherick House on the market. The upkeep is quite a drain on his resources, but he is obliged to spend a certain amount every year on it."

"This house in Truro. The address wouldn't have been ninety-seven Lemon Street, would it?"

"Yes, that's quite right. How did you know?"

"No matter. I'd like to get back to this Mr. Adderstone. I'd like his address and telephone."

"I'm not sure that . . ."

Raleigh said nothing, but the look that passed between him and Pentreath was enough. The solicitor wrote the details on a slip of paper and passed them across the desk. As he did so I turned to him.

"There's something I'd like to know," I said. "Do you have any idea why your Mr. Adderstone refused to let anybody rent the house? Or why he never lived there himself?"

He did not answer at once. Perhaps he was trying to remember a standard reply, perhaps he was trying to invent something of his own. But in the end he just told the truth, what he knew of it.

"He lived there briefly," he said. "With his first wife. She . . ." He hesitated. "She disappeared there one night and was never seen again. He shut the place up after that and never went back."

CHAPTER 11

THE NEXT DAY I drove over to Tredannack. The parish church and its grounds lay on the northern edge of the village, with a magnificent view across fields to the sea. I passed through a low lych-gate and found myself on a winding gravel path. It led to an arched door set in a wide porch. On either side flowers grew, well tended and laid in carefully arranged patterns: monbretias, primulas, columbines, cyclamens. The church was medieval, built of rough gray stone and bearing a tower typical of the region: tall and square, with a pointed pinnacle at each of its four corners.

I skirted the edge of the building, coming on a much narrower path into the churchyard proper. The graves were well looked after, carpeted with grass and summer flowers set in small clumps by a skilled hand. There was some of the beauty of St. Just, but none of the exoticism or the lushness. The newer graves boasted vases, many of them filled with cut flowers. Farther back lay older stones, weathered and leaning at curious angles. I was looking for one dating no farther back than 1953.

It took me longer than I had expected. By guesswork, I stumbled at last on a patch of graves dating back to the right period. Their headstones were stained and discolored, and patched with moss. Tredannack was a small place, and burials in any year were few in number, so I thought I would stumble on Miss Trevorrow quickly enough. In fact, she had not been laid to rest with her friends, if friends she had had. I found her tucked away, single, in a spare corner, far from the other graves, and nearer the old dead than the new. There were no flowers on it, neither planted nor set in a vase. I read the brief inscription.

AGNES TREVORROW
19 December 1869–16 July 1953
"Thou hast removed my soul far off from peace"

The quotation was familiar: it had been taken from the book of Lamentations. *He hath led me, and brought me into darkness, but not into light. . . . He hath set me in dark places, as they that be dead of old. . . . He hath filled me with bitterness, he hath made me drunken with wormwood. . . . And thou hast removed my soul far off from peace.*

It had grown cold. The tall churchyard trees cast deep shadows over the graves, and there was no sunshine where I stood. Far away from me, the sea rippled in a light of its own, but I was not buoyed up by it. I could hear the preacher's voice in my father's church, a voice from my childhood: *He hath led me, and brought me into darkness.*

Out of the corner of my eye, I caught sight of a swift movement, a twisting or a turning as of someone moving suddenly in shadow. I looked around, thinking to catch sight of someone watching me, but there was no one. I was quite alone among the quiet graves. But I was sure I had seen a flash of black clothing, a white face. I left the old grave and turned back to the path.

All that night there were muffled sounds outside my room in Marazion.

The next day I returned to London. Raleigh said he had no further use for me at that point. What, after all, had we accomplished? We had discovered that Sarah had either been in touch with or intended getting in touch with a woman who had been dead for nearly forty years. That made no sense, at least not the sort of sense that would help the police track down a missing person. Or pursue a murder inquiry, if that was what this had become.

Raleigh had latched onto the idea that someone had been playing games with Sarah, using the name Trevorrow and the address of a house in which the real Agnes Trevorrow had lived at different times. Perhaps it was someone who knew of Sarah's fear of Petherick House, someone who thought they could have some fun or make some money by scaring her further. But who this prankster could be or what their real motive may have been were matters not even Raleigh could begin to guess at.

The information about Adderstone and his wife had made an impression on the chief inspector, and he told me that he had asked the Yorkshire police to make inquiries. It was rather too much to expect that Adderstone himself had been involved in Sarah's disappearance; for one thing, young Medawar had been careful to keep our presence at the house a dark secret. He was in custody now, but he had nothing to tell the police that was not banal or self-justifying.

I did not think that for me to stay on in Cornwall would be of material help in the search for Sarah. If she was still alive, I doubted very much that she would have stayed on in the county. A few weeks of rural life, and Sarah would have hared back to her old haunts in the city. She was a city girl at heart. So I headed for London.

After so long on my own, it was a relief to see Tim and Susan. We had a tearful reunion followed by dinner and plenty to drink. They put me to bed afterward, and in the morning Susan said I could stay with them for a while if it would help. I said no and went home shortly afterward.

The flat was just as I had left it. As *we* had left it. There was no sign anywhere of Sarah's having returned even briefly. Without her, the place felt alien and unwelcoming. The familiar rooms had become hostile to my presence. I found myself looking over my shoulder, or listening for sounds in another part of the flat.

I got out the box containing the typed pages I had brought back with me from Cornwall. There were more than enough stories to send to Alan Furst, my editor at Klein Morrow. I added a letter and took the packet to the post office in the next street. While waiting in the line, I again had that uncomfortable feeling that I was being watched, but when I looked around, the little office was empty.

The evening passed tediously and a little unpleasantly. I could not shake off the sense that all was not well in the flat. Since living in Cornwall, I had become jumpy. The mere absence of Sarah made the flat seem queer and inhospitable. All the time, wherever I was, I felt sure that the door of whatever room I was in would open and she would walk in. In a sense, the whole place was already haunted by her, by her sounds and smells, by her having been there for so long and with such intensity.

I slept on my side of the bed, feeling the lack of Sarah more than ever that night. Sleep arrived after much difficulty and was accompanied by dreams. I woke at 3:00 A.M., screaming. For a long time afterward, I lay awake, waiting for something that did not come. Not that night.

Next morning I rang Susan and asked if I could move in after all. Just for a few days, I said, until I could settle down.

"Only if you make yourself useful," she said. "There are to be no artistic tantrums or alcoholic blackouts. You are to arrive home at a reasonable hour. There is to be no typing in your room after midnight. And you will help me with my daughter. Those are my conditions. They are not negotiable."

"I don't have blackouts."

"You come close. The night before last was not the first time."

"You were both drunk as well."

"But not plastered. You were the one that had to be put to bed. You were not a pretty sight."

I caved in. I needed her trust after all. We both knew that. I had no room for negotiation.

"Very well," I said. "I agree. It's only for a few days anyway. Until . . ."

I trailed off.

"Yes, Peter? Until what?"

What had I been on the verge of saying? "Until Sarah comes back?" Did I still believe that?

"Until I can face this place on my own," I stumbled. "That's all."

Susan and I went back a long way. Sometimes it seemed like forever. We had met at university, had even been lovers briefly. Tim knew all about our short, repressed affair. He had not known Susan then, nor I Sarah. Tim had supplanted me, and I had gone on to a succession of short-lived arrangements with other women until Sarah entered my life.

We had met on some dreadful Arts Council committee, a half-baked scheme to combine the talents of painters, writers, and morris dancers, if I remember. I was a teacher then, and had been appointed to the committee by my local education authority to coordinate work in schools. Sarah became my only reason for attending meetings after the first disastrous get-together. The committee fell apart at its third or fourth session, but by then I had taken steps to insure continuity for Sarah and myself. We were, I think, the only real alliance that ever came out of that dreary experiment.

For some reason, the four of us—Susan and Tim, Sarah and I—had become firm friends. I had never quite given up on Susan. I don't mean as a lover—she had long since made clear to me her feelings on that score—but as a friend and counselor. She put up with me and became a close ally of Sarah, especially after Catherine's death. Their friendship and understanding had helped us survive that tragedy.

Tim and I were not really very alike, but soon after our first meeting we discovered a mutual interest in French realist chansons of the twenties and thirties. We would sit and play recordings of Mistinguett and Lucienne Boyer long into the night. Our favorite song was Boyer's "Parlez-moi d'Amour." We would put it on the turntable, light thin cigarettes, and close our eyes. Later, when things were not so good, I would talk about Sarah and what was going wrong with my life. As often as not, Sarah would be upstairs with Susan, doing much the same. He helped me write my first book. In a way, he helped me find myself.

"I'll be there in half an hour," I said, and put the phone down.

Now it is time to mention Rachel, Susan's daughter. Rachel was four years old, quick-witted, unspoiled, beautiful in a way that caught in my throat. Some children are like kittens or puppies: half-formed, lisping creatures with large eyes, overzealous to please. Rachel was already something complete. Not a small adult, never precocious; just complete in and of herself. We knew it was a temporary state, that she might never keep the charm we now enjoyed in her. But while it lasted who could pass Rachel by without stopping heart in mouth, without being altered? She turned heads, and when she was older, she would turn them again. It was not mere prettiness or even beauty, though I would have said she was the most beautiful child I had ever seen: it was because she was present to the onlooker, a whole, undiminished thing.

I spent most of that day in the park with Rachel. Susan was grateful to have a little time alone. She had a piece to write, something about neofascists in Manchester or Hull. It frightened me a little how easily Rachel took my mind off all that happened in Cornwall. We had told her that Sarah was staying down there a little longer, and she had accepted it as children will. She was crazy with energy, I could not take my eyes off her for a moment. Now on the swings, now on the slide, now on the merry-go-round: she made the day sing.

In the afternoon, I took her for tea. Well, tea for me, cake and orange juice for her. We talked and talked. Her conversational skills were limited, but what she lacked in vocabulary or knowledge of the world, she more than made up for with enthusiasm. I remember nothing now of what we talked about. There were no tantrums, no displays of greed or spite. People looked in our direction, smiling; they thought Rachel was my daughter, and I was content for them to think so.

That night, after Rachel was put to bed, Tim and I talked. Susan was out at a political meeting of some sort, part of the research for her series on the British right in the nineties. I told Tim everything, all the details I had left out the night before. There was beer, but I did not touch it, I knew I needed to stay sober for what I had to say. Tim listened; he had always been a good listener. I told him about Margaret Trebarvah and the things she had said to Sarah and, later, to me; about the sounds in the house, Sarah's hat torn to shreds, the child on the tape, the deepening mystery that surrounded Agnes Trevorrow and the house in which she had once lived. Tim listened in silence, pausing only to drink at times from the glass of beer in front of him.

There was already an understanding, I think, that Susan should know nothing of this. She had a hatred of things supernatural that was born in part of her innate skepticism, and in part of fear. Once, when we were sleeping together, I had offered to take her to see *The Exorcist* and she had refused. She pretended not to take such matters seriously, but I suspected that quite the opposite was true, that she had once seen or heard something that had left her fearful.

Before going to bed, I looked in on Rachel. She was

fast asleep. A toy monkey lay on the pillow beside her. His name was Morris. Sarah and I had bought it for her before leaving for Cornwall. I kissed her on the cheek and went to my room.

Later, I was wakened by the muffled sound of Tim and Sarah making love. I turned over and tried to regain sleep, but I could not. I felt alone and confused.

CHAPTER 12

PETHERICK HOUSE HAD started to feel like a bad dream. There were no slamming doors in Tim and Susan's house, no babies crying when they should not be there at all. I was feeling safe for the first time in months. Only Sarah's disappearance lay over me like a shadow betokening a deeper darkness. And then, the very next morning, I was plunged back into the horror.

The phone rang while I was washing up after breakfast. Rachel was watching television in the sitting room. I recognized the voice at once: it was Alan, my editor.

"Peter, how are you feeling?"

"Not too bad. How'd you know I was here?"

"You left the number on your answering machine."

"Did I? I can't remember."

"Peter, what's this about Sarah? You say she's vanished. Has she left you, is that it?"

I explained briefly. There was silence at the other end, then Alan's voice again, subdued.

"I'm sorry, Peter. My God, what can I say? Except that I hope she turns up soon."

"No, Alan, she won't turn up. Not like that, anyway. Sarah's dead. I'm beginning to accept that."

"But surely, without a body . . ."

"It's just a matter of time. That's what they told me. They'll find her. In the end they'll find her."

Another silence. I waited. On the street outside, a group of children played. Their voices were high and resonant. I could hear my own breathing. Alan cleared his throat and continued.

"Peter, in a way it's a bit of a relief to hear what you've just told me."

"That Sarah's dead?"

He stammered, "No . . . no, I . . . I didn't mean that. Quite the opposite. But . . . Well, it explains something that's been worrying me."

He paused.

"Yes?"

"Well," he went on, "I imagine you've been preoccupied, that you've hardly been yourself these past few weeks."

"I don't understand, Alan. What are you trying to say?"

"Well, it's these stories, Peter—the ones you sent me."

"What's wrong with them? Don't you like them? For God's sake, Alan, they're the best thing I've written in years. I was back on my old form."

A protracted silence.

"Peter, maybe it's just a simple mistake. Have you started using a word processor?"

"Of course not. You know my feelings about computers. I typed every page out with my own dainty fingers."

"Every page?"

"Obviously."

"In that case, how come all you've sent me is twenty copies of the same piece?"

I felt myself go cold.

"I'm sorry, Alan," I said. "I don't think I understand. I sent you everything I had in my box from Cornwall. There was one set of carbons, which I've still got at the flat. I made no photocopies. What you have is twenty separate stories. Maybe your secretary tried to copy them and made a hash of it."

"Corinne hasn't even seen them. She's off ill. What I have, Peter, is twenty identical copies of a document which isn't even a story. It looks more like the transcript of an inquest. The style is late Victorian English. It could be part of a story, I suppose, but it's a bit on the long side."

The room seemed to spin. I thought of Sarah and her paintings, the ones she had done at Petherick House, so alike, yet so dissimilar in one particular.

"That's impossible," I said.

"Why don't you check?" said Alan. "Get back to me once you've sorted it out. And don't worry about it. From the sound of it, you've been under a lot of strain, Peter. A hell of a lot. You're entitled to a few cock-ups."

But it had not been a cock-up, and I think Alan knew it. He knew my working methods as well as I did. I had never been anything but careful and methodical. I did not make unconsidered slips.

I drove back to my flat. The box of carbons was where I had left it, beneath my desk. I went through them one page at a time. It took me about two hours. By the time I had finished, I was sweating. Alan had been right: what I had was a single document repeated again and again.

Later, when I was able to examine the repetitions in greater detail, I found that they were not, in fact, exact reproductions one of the other. Like Sarah's paintings, they contained minor differences—a word here, an emphasis there, a phrase dropped, a sentence added, an expression altered. But the sense never changed.

As Alan had thought, it was the transcript of an inquest, or a fragment of one. Each time it opened and ended in the middle of a sentence, always at the same point, as though it had at one instant erupted into my mind and installed itself there like a worm, creeping in slow circles through it, as through the heart of a green apple:

. . . has now been positively identified. The remains are those of Miss Susannah Trevorrow, spinster, aged twenty-two, of Petherick House in the parish of Tredannack, here adjacent. Identification was made by her sister, Miss Agnes Trevorrow, likewise a spinster, of the same address. The deceased was reported missing by her sister on the sixteenth of July, the day after her disappearance, and a little more than three months before the discovery of her body on the Zawn Quoit rocks, below Trowan Cliff, west of St. Ives. The body was found on the morning of the twenty-fifth of October, following the great storm of the previous night. It was in a state of advanced decay and was thought unrecognizable, but by good fortune a jet bracelet had remained fastened to the corpse's left wrist. It was by means of this bracelet that Miss Agnes Trevorrow was able to effect recognition of her lamented sister's remains.

This bracelet had indeed been given to Susannah Trevorrow by her sister Agnes on the occasion of her fifteenth birthday, and was inscribed with her initials, namely S. T., the letters incised within a circle and still perfectly visible. Both parents of the missing woman being dead, Miss Agnes Trevorrow attended the coroner's office of St. Ives on the twenty-sixth of October. There, she was shown her sister's bracelet, which she identified. Having done this, she was overcome with grief, and was subsequently confined to bed by Dr. Gibney, her attendant physician.

In the course of the inquest, it was revealed by the coroner that the deceased showed signs of having given birth to a child some three to four years previously. When questioned about this, Agnes Trevorrow admitted that it was true her sister had conceived and borne a female child in September 1883, and that this child was now a little above four years of age. Who the father had been was not known, nor was likely now to be, for Susannah Trevorrow had at all times refused to reveal his identity. In order to avoid the scandal that would necessarily have attended this sorry event, the child had been placed with an orphanage in another part of the county immediately after birth, and was thought either to be there still or to have been adopted. As is not uncommon in such cases, the mother was told that her child had died soon after its delivery. It would appear that the father of the dead woman, Mr. Jeremiah Trevorrow, a gentleman farmer, had died on the fifth of February of this year, and that Miss Trevorrow, already in a depressed state of mind following the supposed death of her child, went rapidly into a further decline.

It was the opinion of Agnes Trevorrow that her sister, weighed down by this double grief and no longer able to contain her feelings, took steps to end her own life by casting herself from the high cliff that lies only yards from Petherick House.

In view of the circumstances, the coroner, Mr. Worthy, directed that no further questions be directed to Miss Trevorrow, and that the matter of the child not be reported in the public press. Nor was it considered necessary to conduct further inquiries concerning the fate of the child of the deceased woman, this being held not material to the case.

A verdict of death by suicide was recorded, and permission was given for the burial of the remains in the public ground at St. Ives. In the course of the inquest, the following witnesses were brought to give testimony. . . .

The rest of the document provided a more detailed account of the proceedings, with transcriptions of various depositions given by the police, the fisherman who had found Susannah Trevorrow's body, the physician who had carried out the autopsy, and Agnes Trevorrow herself.

I read it all, not once, but several times, as though in search of something. What had I been thinking of when I wrote it? I still had my list of ideas, the ones I had set out to work on while in Cornwall. None bore the slightest resemblance to this. But I did not have to look far for my inspiration: Petherick House, the cliff, a missing woman, Agnes Trevorrow. Together, they had bewitched me.

That night Rachel woke screaming from a nightmare. I heard her cry out, then the sound of her sobbing, and moments later Susan's footsteps on the way to her room. She was soon quieted. I lay awake long afterward, fearing my own dreams.

In the morning, I asked Susan what had happened.

"She had a bad dream, that's all."

"Did she say what it was about?"

Susan shook her head.

"No, she wouldn't say. She seemed badly frightened, though."

She paused to sip her coffee. I thought she looked tired. There were rings below her eyes.

"There was one thing, though." She looked at me thoughtfully. "She kept telling me she didn't want to go back. I asked her 'back where?' but she wouldn't or couldn't say. I can't think where she means. You don't have any idea, do you, Peter?"

I said no and left the table. In the garden, Rachel was playing with her dolls. Early sunlight lay on her. She looked up at me and smiled. I smiled back, but as I did so the sunlight faded and a shadow fell across the garden.

CHAPTER 13

IT WAS NOT until the evening that I remembered that the sixteenth of July—the day on which Susannah Trevorrow had disappeared in 1887—had also been the date of Sarah's disappearance. And according to the gravestone I had seen in Tredannack, the very day on which Agnes Trevorrow had died in 1953. I could no longer doubt that something in the past, something that had happened in Petherick House all those years ago, had drawn Sarah back to itself. Or reached out for her in the present.

I wrote to Raleigh, telling him of my little discovery and enclosing a copy of the inquest report. Would he, I asked, check the police files for that year to see if there was anything further on the death of Susannah Trevorrow? I was not convinced that the evidence given by Agnes had been true or complete, though I could not say in what particulars I doubted her. It was just that whatever had happened in that house had left a legacy of deep disturbance, and I did not think a simple suicide explained all I had seen and heard and felt there.

While waiting for Raleigh's reply, I started writing again, slowly and painfully, with none of the élan I had felt in Cornwall. Every few days I would show what I had written to Tim. He reassured me that I was no longer deluding myself, that what I had penned was fiction of my own making and not some incubus from the past.

My dreams continued no less intensely than before. Every night now, sometimes twice. The empty house seemed alive with presences. One night—it must have been the tenth or eleventh of September—I found myself at the top of the stairs on the second floor. As I turned the corner to pass into the corridor, I twisted around and looked back. On the stairs behind me, near the bottom, a small figure was standing, staring up at me. We looked at one another for a very long time. Neither of us said a word. I guessed her to be about four years old. Her face was very pale. She had dark, hollow eyes. Once, she seemed to be speaking, but when her mouth opened, no sounds came from it. I closed my eyes. When I opened them again, she was gone. A door slammed hard, and I woke, covered in thick sweat and shivering.

I am ten years older now. My hair is white. My right hand trembles sometimes when I write, and I have to stop until it grows still. I know so much and so little.

Last week, they buried Alan Furst. The funeral was near Norwich, where he had grown up, in a church-yard planted with willows. His grave was newly dug, a narrow opening at the foot of a tall yew tree. The weather was black and cold, we were a bleak, wind-swept collection of mourners huddled about the grave. His wife and daughters were there in black, some people I knew from the publishing house, other authors come to say their good-byes. I watched from a distance as they lowered him. There were crows on the branches of the tree.

When will it be my turn? Will there be a yew tree? Will anyone come to see me laid to rest? But I do not think that even then I shall have true rest.

Raleigh took over a week to answer my letter. I did not recognize him in his writing. He adopted a formal, pedantic style, one at odds with the rough and direct manner that he used in person. Beneath the professional formality, I detected something else—an evasiveness, a sense of misdirection or concealment that again seemed alien. Behind his stilted wariness, I sensed that he was worried about something, but that he could not bring himself to tell me what it was.

He had dug up a heap of old files from both police and coroner's archives, but they said little that I did not know already. How had I found out about the case in the first place? he asked. The transcript I had sent him had been an almost verbatim copy of the original inquest report. In my letter, I had avoided telling him how I had come by my information, and now I felt myself trapped by my own lack of candor. How, after all, could I explain that my hand had been guided by a force outside myself, that I had never seen a report of the inquest or even known that it existed? It was something I could barely admit even to myself.

One fragment of fresh information did emerge, however. In one of the police files, Raleigh had discovered a short report appended to the coroner's summary. It had been written by James Curry, the parish constable at Tredannack. According to Curry, local gossip had it that Susannah Trevorrow had given birth to a girl child four years earlier and that, as far as anyone knew, this child had still been alive and living at Petherick House until the time of her mother's disappearance. People said her name was Catherine or Katy—no one knew for certain. I remembered with a shudder the voice I had heard in Petherick House, calling that same name.

A second rumor maintained that the child's father had been none other than Jeremiah Trevorrow, Susannah's father. Curry was inclined to dismiss the rumors about the father as malicious. Jeremiah Trevorrow had not been a popular man. He was notorious for underpaying his farm laborers, and abrupt dismissals for small misdemeanors had always been the rule on his lands. The policeman visited the house himself and was shown around by Agnes, but there had been no sign of a child or a child's belongings in any of the rooms he had entered.

Sarah's parents came down to pay me a visit on the nineteenth. We had a tense meeting that all but ended in accusations of my having done away with Sarah, and I found it hard to restrain myself from striking her father. He was the same sniveling little brute he had always been. I had never learned to love, much less to respect him. Her mother, whom I still called Mrs. Trevor to her face, wore her sour, saintly expression throughout, wringing her thin hands and muttering platitudes. She left in tears. I had no comfort for them. Sarah was missing, probably dead: that was all I knew.

I did not tell them anything about Petherick House

or any of the things that had happened there. To have done so would only have served to confirm their suspicions. I imagine they would have demanded that Raleigh be taken off the case, just when I needed him most.

He wrote to me again, a week after that first letter. There was no fresh information, he said. All his trails had dried up, he was beginning to lose hope again. The Yorkshire police had drawn a blank with Richard Adderstone. He had been unable to tell them anything of value. Raleigh wondered if I thought it worthwhile for him to travel north in order to interview Adderstone in person.

The letter was strange, written in a crabbed, obsessive hand, with tall, fencelike letters strangely spaced.

I go to Petherick House every day now [he wrote] though I never enter. It is very quiet there. The leaves have started to fall in the garden. The house is sad, and at times angry. I walk down to the cliff top and look out across the sea. Sometimes wind crosses it. There are gulls in the garden, and at times their crying reminds me of a child in tears. When I look back at the house from there, I can see rows of windows. Sometimes I think I am being watched.

Last night I dreamed of your wife, Sarah. She has been in my dreams for seven weeks now, almost every night. I recognize her from the photograph you left. She never speaks to me. She is constantly silent, and she stares at me with dreaming eyes. If she spoke to me, what would she say? Do you know? Can you guess?

No, I could not guess. We had never been that close, Sarah and I. We had loved one another, but I had never learned what was in her heart, I had never penetrated that deeply. And now it was too late. One thing, however, I did not understand. It made me bitter. Why Raleigh? Why not me?

Dreams were not enough. Work was not enough. The long dead weeks dragged unbearably. Autumn came like a weight. I had no focus for my life or thoughts, no way of closing what was past. My one consolation was Rachel. During those early-autumn weeks, Susan was much preoccupied with work. There had been riots in Birmingham and Bradford, followed by exchanges on the floor of the House on the need to clamp down harder on the extreme right. An anti-fascist demonstration in Manchester had ended in the death of a student. His killers were still at large. One of the national dailies asked Susan to do a short series, then a major Sunday asked her to travel around the riot scenes with a photographer. Rachel became my exclusive charge for days at a time.

We watched television together. Postman Pat, Juniper Jungle, Jackanory. I told her about the programs I had watched when I was a child. My favorites had been Bill and Ben, the Flowerpot Men. Rachel fell about laughing when I did my voices for Weed or for Bill speaking to Slowcoach the Tortoise: "Huddo, Sluggalug." I made her breakfast, lunch, and late tea, which we ate together in the kitchen. When I needed to work, she would play silently with her dolls or watch a video. I tried teaching her to read, and found to my amazement that she could pick up simple words with ease. Writing proved more difficult, for she still lacked the coordination needed to manipulate a pen correctly; but with a little help she was nevertheless able to write short notes to Susan, telling her her news. We put the notes in impressive envelopes and took them to the mailbox at the end of the road, where I lifted Rachel while she posted them.

As far as possible, however, I avoided venturing outdoors. On several occasions—once near the swings in the park, twice on the High Street, once in the supermarket—I had caught a glimpse of a figure dressed in black, watching us. Each time it had been gone when I looked again, but I did not think I had been mistaken.

"I don't like it when Mummy goes away," said Rachel one day as she sat beside me, drawing with crayons I had just bought for her.

"But she'll be back tomorrow," I said. "And Daddy will be home early tonight."

She shook her head.

"I don't have a daddy," she said, quite matter-of-factly.

"Nonsense. You have a very nice daddy."

She frowned, as though uncertain of something.

"Well," she said finally, "I didn't before."

"Before?" I smiled. "What do you mean?"

"Before I was born," she said. She was still frowning, creasing her eyes as though in an effort to make sense of something, or to remember.

"I don't understand," I said.

"Before," she said. "Before I was Rachel. When I lived in a big house."

"When was this?" I asked. "I thought you'd always lived here."

"No," she said, shaking her head. Her little face was quite tense, the expression on it wholly serious. I could see that it would hurt if I made fun of her. And for some reason I did not want to, not even gently.

"Where did you live then?"

"I told you. In a big old house. Not like this one at all. It had a garden all 'round it. A garden with trees, like in the park. And if you went through the garden, you could see the sea."

I felt my skin go cold.

"Rachel," I said, "you're making this up, aren't you?"

"Don't call me that," she said. "That's not my name."

"But of course it is," I said. "You've always been Rachel."

But inside I was feeling terribly afraid.

She shook her head slowly.

"No," she said. "I can't remember very well, but I wasn't called Rachel when I lived in the big house."

"What were you called? Can you remember?"

"You know," she said. "You know what I was called."

My breath was tight in my chest. I scarcely dared speak.

"No," I said. "I don't know. Why don't you tell me?"

She looked directly at me. She had such big eyes, such haunted eyes.

"Catherine," she said. "I was called Catherine. And I lived in a big house near the sea. The house had a name, too."

"Can you remember what it was called?"

"It was a long name," she said. "I'm not sure. Maybe it was Peter House. Like your name."

"Peter?"

I could feel the pool of horror stirring in me. They were still clutching out from their past.

"Something like that," she said. "Longer than that."

"Petherick?" I asked, sick. "Was that it, Rachel? Was it Petherick?"

A smile lit her face, then a half-frightened look crossed it.

"Yes," she said, half in a whisper. "That was what we called it. I had a kitten then."

*   *   *

Early the next day I had a call from Raleigh. They had found a body. At the foot of steep cliffs to the west of St. Ives. The body of a woman, long-drowned.

I scarcely listened. I was tired. All the night before, Rachel had been screaming.

CHAPTER 14

BY THE TIME I left for St. Ives, Rachel seemed herself again. I was anxious for her, but I felt there was nothing I could say to Tim about what I knew. If I were to voice my suspicions, he would have little choice but to ask me to leave for good. Far better I stayed there, where I could keep an eye on her. After breakfast I talked with Rachel, explaining that I had to go away, without saying why. I did not refer to our conversation of the previous day: she needed to sleep without dreams.

I took the midmorning train to Penzance. All the way down I watched through a rain-spattered window as the autumn fields rattled past. I could neither read nor write. All I could think about was Sarah lying disfigured in a cold mortuary, or Sarah floating, faceless, in the vast ocean. All around me people were talking or reading, living their lives in the limbo that lay between departure and arrival. Depending on class and taste, they read *The Sun* or *Hello!* or the latest Booker Prize winner. They had left loved ones behind, or would be met by others at the station. I was different. My wife had been washed up on the seashore like just another piece of jetsam. I would never speak to her again.

Sarah's disappearance had cast me into a limbo of my own. But now I was coming down to earth. At last, I thought, it would all end. I looked out on newly harvested farmlands, at the long, sealike expanse of the sky. Then the sea itself lay on my left, and we were pulling into Penzance. My journey was almost over.

Raleigh himself was waiting for me at the station. He had changed. Something vital had gone out of him. I thought he looked ill.

"I've got a car waiting outside," he said. "They're expecting us at the coroner's office."

"You haven't asked me how I am," I said.

"I've not time for that. Let's get this thing over."

"It is her?" I asked. "You're sure of that?"

He said nothing, turning and going ahead of me, not even looking to see if I was following. His sergeant had not come with him. I tossed my overnight bag into the back. Raleigh wanted me to stay down for the inquest. He took the wheel and nipped out into the traffic.

We had been driving for about a minute when he turned to me.

"Who else could it be?" he asked.

"I don't understand."

"Mr. Clare, your wife went missing in July. In the period between then and now, no female bodies have been found in this region. The body at Zawn Quoits is the first. It's not in good condition, and you won't be asked to look at it."

"Then why have you brought me down?"

"It's a formality. We are sure it's your wife. If you agree, you'll be given legal charge of her remains, for burial or cremation."

"I can get Sarah's dental records," I said. "If that would help."

He did not answer at once. I noticed that his hands were tight on the wheel, that his knuckles were white. We were driving along the promenade, with the sea on our left, cold and driven.

"No," he said. "They'd be no help. The face was . . . badly disfigured. The lower jaw is completely gone. And the top . . . Better not think of it."

But I could not help thinking of it. I had once kissed her, after all. His corpse had been my lover.

"There was a little hair," he said, "at the back of the skull. We had some strands of your wife's hair that we took from her pillow. I had them compared. The forensic lab says they're satisfied the strands are identical." He paused. "There's just one thing."

"What's that?"

"It'll wait," he said. "We're nearly there."

We turned right onto Lidden Road. Moments later we drew up outside the coroner's office. They were waiting for us. The assistant coroner, a man called Hawkes, greeted us morosely. He shook my hand.

"This is just a formality, you understand, Mr. Clare. The remains we believe to be your wife's are being kept in the mortuary at West Cornwall Hospital here in Penzance, where they were brought by Coastguard Cliff Rescue. Since they are badly decomposed, we do not expect you to view them. Perhaps Chief Inspector Raleigh has explained. . . ."

His voice trailed away, as though trained to do so. He was a tidy man with watery blue eyes and pale, aching skin. Something beneath the surface threatened to break out. He was a churchgoer, perhaps, or a frequenter of pornographic cinemas. I sensed something furtive and inwardly angry about him.

"Yes," I said. "He's told me all about it."

"Good," he muttered, "very good. Now, the inquest itself will be tomorrow. As the chief inspector will have explained, we have decided to hold it in St. Ives rather than here or Camborne. This is in case anyone should wish to visit the spot where your wife is thought to have fallen to her death or the place where the remains were found, although I have to say that I think neither is very likely."

He paused.

"I have some papers I'd like you to sign. Why don't you step inside and sit down while we go through all this?"

I followed him. Raleigh had gone ahead of us. Photographs of the hair strands were shown to me, together with wooden descriptions of the laboratory analysis that had found them identical. It seemed enough. I declared myself satisfied.

"There's one thing more," said Hawkes. I saw Raleigh watching me. His face was expressionless.

Hawkes reached into a drawer and took from it a small white cardboard box. He removed the lid and reached inside.

"Tell me, Mr. Clare," he said, "do you recognize this?"

In his hand he held a bracelet. A black bracelet carved with little flowers. I guessed that it was made of jet. It reminded me of something.

I shook my head.

"No," I said. "I've never seen it before."

"You're sure it did not belong to your wife? You never saw her wearing it?"

"No," I said. "Never." I remembered now. Susannah Trevorrow had worn a bracelet just like this. Her sister, Agnes, had identified it during the inquest.

Hawkes frowned. Raleigh did not take his eyes off me.

"Mr. Clare, perhaps you can tell me what your wife's initials were."

"Her initials? Why, S.C., of course. She didn't have any middle names."

"And before you were married? What was her maiden name?

"Trevor. Her name was Sarah Trevor."

He pushed the bracelet toward me, holding it up so the light caught it obliquely.

"This bracelet was found on the body at Zawn Quoits," Hawkes said.

On the side facing me were two initials set in a circle. I did not have to strain to see what they were. S. T.

Raleigh had reserved a room for me in a hotel at St. Ives. The road along which we drove had been drenched with sunshine when I last saw it. Now the trees dripped with rain and the light was colorless. Raleigh had a short fit of coughing. When it passed, I turned to him. I had been thinking of Hawkes's words, about someone wanting to inspect the place where Sarah's body had been found.

"How far is it from here to where she was washed up?"

"Zawn Quoits? Not far. A few minutes' drive. But you'd have to walk the last bit."

"Could we go there first? I'd like to see it while there's still light."

He glanced at his watch, then nodded.

We left the car at a place called Higher Burthallan and set off on foot. The sea air seemed to set off Raleigh's cough again. The sky above us was filled with kittiwakes, driven inland by a storm at sea. There was a stiff breeze and rain that lashed our faces as we walked. A footpath took us down to Hellesveor Cliff, where we struck due west on a narrow path that skirted the shore. On either side of us the land was bleak and open. We passed gray stone outcrops and fields of bracken turning brown. No trees grew here, only gorse and stunted hawthorn bushes. It was not a long walk. A few minutes later Raleigh took my arm, holding me fast.

"Here," he said. "These are the Trowan Cliffs. The Zawn Quoits are below."

I looked down. The sound of waves hitting the shore reminded me of the cliff at Petherick House. It was the same coastline, the same rocks. I shivered at the thought of falling, at the thought of lying, naked and exposed, on such a cold bed. It was a lonely place to be driven to by the tides.

"The fishermen say the currents would have taken her out, then back again in the storm." Raleigh's voice was unstable, shaken by the wind. He coughed hard, bringing up phlegm. Beneath us, the waves sluiced the rocks.

"Was she there long?" I asked.

He shook his head.

"They found her the day after the storm. Not long."

"This is where Susannah Trevorrow was found, wasn't it?"

"Yes," he said. He seemed ill at ease. "It makes sense. The currents won't have changed much since her day."

He turned to me.

"Have you seen what you came to see?"

I nodded. I was still trying to imagine what it meant to be naked and alone down there, to be nothing more than a thing the sea had coughed up.

CHAPTER

I SPENT THE EVENING in the Garrack Hotel, where Raleigh had reserved a room for me. My window looked out toward the shore between Clodgy Point and the headland at Porthmeor Beach, with the sea beyond. Trowan Cliffs were just out of sight, a little to the west. Perhaps it was not the best of views that night, perhaps what happened later would not have occurred had I not found myself sitting there in my room, staring at the sea and thinking. Raleigh had gone home to his wife. I had suggested dinner, but he wanted to keep things businesslike, he said. All the same, his company would have helped; I might not have brooded quite so much.

I went out about one in the morning. By then I knew there was little point in trying to sleep. If someone had stopped me and asked where I was headed, I would have told them I was going for a stroll. As far as I know, that was all there was in my mind at that time. Just a walk to the shore and back. The sea air would clear my head and help me to sleep.

The weather was still rough, with stiffening squalls that tore across the rooftops and hammered through the narrow, twisting streets. For a few moments I would find myself in shelter, then I would turn a corner and the wind would snap at me again. On any other night, I would have turned and headed back indoors. I passed no one on the street. St. Ives is always a quiet place, and all the more so out of season.

On the northern edge of the town, a steep hill leads down to Porthmeor Beach. The sands are flanked higher up on the land side by a stretch of sheltered ground with cafés, toilets, and a putting green. Next to that there is a cemetery and a car park. It was only when I saw the graveyard name in the light of a street lamp that I realized where I was.

According to the papers found by Raleigh, Barnoon Cemetery was where Susannah Trevorrow had been buried. Had I stumbled there by chance, blown to the spot by the wind, or had it been my intention to head there all along?

I stood for a while, straining in the darkness to make out the jumble of graves behind the fence. It was no good. I would need a flashlight. My first thought was to try a shed in one of the gardens in West Place, just behind me. But then I remembered that the cemetery chapel was divided into two sections and that the building joining them was a store. I might find a flashlight there.

It proved very easy. The doors to the chapel store faced seaward and were not overlooked. A heavy stone broke the padlock at the second or third blow. I had to fumble about in the darkness for a while, but I found what I was looking for. A large rubber flashlight lay on a shelf among trowels, forks, and gardening gloves. I decided to borrow it for a few minutes in order to look for the grave. It would be a matter of moments to replace it afterward.

It was as I was leaving that I noticed the spades. The beam of the flashlight fell on them as I lit my way to the door. Had that been in my mind from the start as well? I hesitated for only a moment, then snatched a spade from the stack and went back into the night.

Even with the help of the flashlight, it was difficult work stumbling about among the tumbled graves. I discovered that the cemetery had been built on three terraces, divided by rough stone walls, and that the ground dropped away steeply between them. The first level consisted of a mixture of graves dating from around the end of the last century to the present day. A rapid tour of the older graves revealed nothing of interest.

I crossed to the second level and started to work my way up and down. The wind tugged at me, fresh from the sea. The names of the dead flickered in the light of the torch, their chiseled edges worn down by years of exposure. I could not even be sure there had been a headstone or, if there had been, that it still stood.

But I was not disappointed. The Trevorrows had been wealthy in their way, and Agnes had evidently spent not a little on her sister's monument. It was a marble pillar topped by a draped urn. I could see that it had not been tended in a long time, and that the elements had worn it down. Seaside gravestones are often eaten away by the salt. But the marble of Susannah Trevorrow's resting place had withstood storm and sea spray better than most of the headstones around it. Her name was still legible, and so, too, was the inscription beneath:

SUSANNAH TREVORROW
27 February 1865–16 July 1887
"The sea shall give up its dead"

I switched off the flashlight and set to work. The grave was grown over with fibrous seaside grass, through which I had to cut my way before reaching the soil beneath. Fortunately, the earth itself was fairly light and sandy on top, and I made good progress. The grave was set far down on the second terrace, out of view from the road, and I was able to conceal the light well enough behind the stone. The spade went deep at every thrust. I dug like someone demented, far into the night. From time to time I thought I heard sounds around me, voices, perhaps, or something running through the thick grass. But I did not look up. It's just the wind, I told myself.

They had not buried her deep. Perhaps Agnes had wanted it that way. I hardly know. My spade struck the coffin lid in the third hour of digging. I used the flashlight to confirm that what I had reached was wood. Even with the wind, it had seemed a loud sound. I had a madness on me that night. I must have had, otherwise I could not have gone through with it.

It took me another half hour to clear the soil properly from the lid. There was a grave stench all around me. I stood to my chest now, my feet balancing on the coffin itself. Cutting the grave back on one side of the coffin, I made a space in which I could stand. When I stepped down into it at last, the edge of the grave came level with my shoulders.

The coffin had been built of hardwood. It had cracked and swollen in places, but the body of it was sound. The lid was still screwed down hard. That was the most difficult job, bending down in that dreadful place, with the light of the torch growing dimmer all the time I worked, forcing the screws back with the edge of the spade, which was my only tool. The screws gave reluctantly, as though determined to guard their trust to the very end. Two snapped clean off, the others twisted from the wood a fraction of an inch at a time.

Even then, it was only with the greatest effort that I could free the lid from the body of the coffin. I had almost no room in which to maneuver, no space to slip the spade between them in an attempt to lever them apart. But I pushed and shoved as well as I could.

The lid gave with a wrenching sound, and keeping my eyes closed, I pushed it across the coffin and up against the side of the grave. It rested there precariously, propped back by the spade. A terrible stench rose from the coffin, making me choke. I tied a handkerchief around my mouth before continuing. Like someone in a dream, I bent down and opened my eyes. In my right hand, the flashlight was shaking as I looked inside.

The grave had finished what the sea had begun. The half skull lay twisted to one side. A few strands of dark hair lay on the stained and rotted pillow beneath it. Already half-decomposed by the action of the salt water, the flesh must have fallen from Susannah's bones rapidly. There was no trace of skin anywhere on the naked skull.

They had covered her in a long shroud. It seemed to be intact, but as I reached out my hand to draw it aside, the cloth, long ago rotted, disintegrated at my touch and uncovered the bones beneath. I shuddered, but I forced myself to go on with what I had started. I had my reasons. Holding my breath, and fighting back my rising horror, I pulled the shreds of fabric away until I had uncovered Susannah's hands.

It was there on her wrist, as I had expected it to be: a jet bracelet. The carving and initials were identical to those on the bracelet I had been shown earlier that day.

Still shaking, I continued to pull the winding cloth apart. But there was nothing more to find. Just white bones and dust.

CHAPTER 16

THE INQUEST DID NOT take long. The evidence for identification was presented by Raleigh. I was not asked to say much: merely to reiterate what I had already told the police concerning Sarah's disappearance on the sixteenth of July. I said nothing about why she might have left the house that night, nor was I pressed to express an opinion.

Sarah's sister, Lorna, had come down from Sheffield to testify. She said Sarah had owned a bracelet like the one found on the body. The family had been on holiday together in Whitby, and Sarah had ordered the bracelet made to her own design in a shop specializing in antique and modern jet ware. I said nothing to challenge Lorna's testimony, but I had never seen Sarah wear such a bracelet.

The evidence concerning the hair strands and testimony regarding the length of time the remains had been in the water clinched the business of identification. The coroner entered a verdict of death by misadventure.

My parents-in-law were there. They were coldly polite and left me in no doubt that they disagreed with the verdict. Raleigh told me later that they had been with him the day before, making veiled accusations. He did not seem to like them. I wondered what they might have told him about me. The truth, probably.

"What about your own parents?" he asked. "I might have thought . . ."

"They're dead," I told him. "Before Sarah and I met. There was an accident."

"I'm sorry. It was none of my business."

Lorna came over to me afterward. She was apologetic and grief-stricken. I think she wanted to use me as a bridge for her feelings about Sarah, as a vehicle for some facile reconciliation. They had never been close, and in recent years Lorna's jealousy of her sister had been like a poison souring everything it touched. I let her vent her guilt, but I refused to let it touch me. I had enough guilt of my own to cope with.

I wanted to ask her about the bracelet, but in the end decided against it. Things were better left as they were.

Raleigh saw me to the station.

"What's wrong?" I asked. "You don't seem well."

He hesitated before answering, as though making his mind up about something.

"You'll hear soon enough," he said. "I'm ill. TB. It started about a month ago."

I looked at him incredulously.

"TB? People don't get TB anymore."

"Don't they? It's happening all the time. There are these new strains, you see. Drug-resistant. All these powerful drugs, they make the bacteria mutate.

That's what I've got, or so they tell me. Mutated frigging bacteria."

"But they can treat you, can't they?"

Raleigh shook his head.

"That's the problem," he said. "These buggers can resist the strongest drugs they've got. I may not have very long. I wanted to find your wife before things took a turn for the worse. We won't have to meet again."

"Do you still dream of her?"

He did not answer at once. I wondered what he felt.

"Every night. I can see her more clearly every time. As though we're getting closer."

"You shouldn't talk like this. You're growing morbid."

"I have reason to." He glanced up.

"Here," he said, "you'd better go or you'll miss your train."

"Did they say much about me?"

"Who?"

"The Trevors. My loving parents-in-law."

He hesitated.

"What you might expect," he said. "It doesn't matter. It makes no difference to anything."

"You're sure of that?"

He nodded and said no more.

"I'm going to Yorkshire," I said. "To see Adderstone."

"No need now. We've found your wife."

"I still want to know. About Agnes Trevorrow."

Raleigh shook his head.

"Leave it alone. It can't do any good."

I took his hand.

"I'll write to you," I said. "Thanks. Thanks for everything."

"Take care," he answered.

Over the PA system came an announcement telling

passengers my train was about to leave. I could see nontravelers stepping onto the platform and closing doors. People were waving from open windows.

"I'd like to stay in touch," I said.

"Yes. Do that. I'll let you know if anything else comes up here."

I headed for the gate. When I got there, I turned and saw him, still watching me. On an impulse, I walked back a few paces toward him.

"Does she ever speak?" I asked.

He looked at me gently and shook his head.

I looked back again as I prepared to board the train. He was no longer there.

Susan was waiting up for me when I got home. Tim had gone to a conference in Birmingham. Rachel was in bed.

"How did it go, Peter? Was it beastly?" Susan was doing her best to keep her feelings in check. She had loved Sarah, possibly more than I had.

I shrugged.

"Not really. Just very dull. It didn't seem to have anything to do with Sarah or me."

"The identification. They didn't make you . . . ?" She shuddered.

I shook my head.

"No," I said. "Nothing like that. It was all done by science. Clean and impersonal."

"That's all right, then, isn't it?" She smiled, then looked away.

I sat down beside her.

"Would you like something?" she asked. "A drink or something?"

"No, thanks. I had a gin on the train. A few gins, actually. But I'm not plastered. Just tired."

"It's all right. You can be forgiven a few gins on a day like today. I've had a few myself. I wish one of us could have gone with you. You could have done with some moral support."

"The Trevors were there. Mum and Dad. He had a dark suit on. And a black tie. Lorna was there as well."

"The awful Lorna? You poor thing."

"She tried to make friends. She means well, I think."

"Don't you believe it." She paused. "Still, it's over now, isn't it?"

"Over?"

"Well, this stage of things. The uncertainty. Have you got a date for the funeral?"

"They're doing all that. The Trevors. I said they could—it's their sort of thing, after all. It's to be in Huddersfield. Some grim municipal cemetery. Victorian angels." I shuddered. I was thinking about the night before. "Will you come with me? To the funeral."

She nodded.

"Of course I will. We'll all be there. Leave it to me, Peter; I'll ring 'round tomorrow." She looked at me. Her eyes had filled with unexpected tears. "Oh, Peter. I still can't believe it's true. Not Sarah . . ."

I put my arm around her, comforting her as best I could. We remained like that for a long time while she cried. I had no tears to add to hers. I had lost mine somewhere along the way.

Finally, she straightened up and wiped her eyes with the back of her hand.

"I'm sorry, Peter. I'm not being much help."

I ran my hand down her back.

"You're more help than you can imagine."

She glanced at me.

"By the way, Peter—I forgot to tell you. A parcel

arrived for you this morning. It's over there on the sideboard."

"Any idea where from?" I asked, getting to my feet. I had not been expecting anything.

Susan shrugged.

"I didn't look."

I crossed to the table and picked up the package, a rectangular box wrapped in brown paper, about two feet long and ten inches wide. The postmark was too blurred to read. There was no sender's name, just my own, written in careful longhand.

The wrapping came off easily. Inside was a stout cardboard box. It held two objects, each wrapped in brown paper. The first seemed to be a tiny box; it had my name written clearly on the outside. The second, much larger, bore Rachel's name. I looked carefully, but there was no sign of a note or card.

"There's something here for Rachel," I said, lifting the large object from the box and handing it to Susan.

While she unwrapped it I tore the paper from the small box in my hand. Inside was a small velvet box, the sort used by jewelers. I could not say whether or not it was familiar, I had seen so many like it. It felt very light. Lifting the small brass clasp, I opened it.

Inside was a ring. A platinum wedding ring. I recognized it without difficulty.

"What is it, Peter?" I heard Susan ask. Her voice sounded far away.

"Sarah's ring," I said quietly. "Her wedding ring."

"It must have been left behind in Cornwall."

"Yes, it must," I lied. I closed the box. The ring had not been left at Petherick House. It had been on Sarah's finger the night of her disappearance, I was certain of it. She had never been known to take it off, not even in a quarrel. I glanced at the box again, feeling the old fear tighten around my heart.

"I don't understand," said Susan. "Why would any-one send this to Rachel?"

I looked up. Susan was holding a doll in her hands. It was a Victorian boy doll, one of those grotesque things with a grown-up's head, dressed in a sailor suit. At first appraisal, it did not seem to be a replica.

Something about the doll made me uneasy. Its little eyes stared at me with an almost malevolent intelli-gence. The face seemed old, not at all childlike. It filled me with revulsion to think of Rachel playing with such a toy: caressing it, introducing it to all her other dolls.

"I can't think who can have sent it," Susan said.

Nor could I. At least . . .

"Maybe a relative . . ." I ventured lamely.

Susan shook her head.

"It's not her birthday or anything. If it came with Sarah's ring . . ." She hesitated. "Perhaps there was someone you met in Cornwall, someone you men-tioned Rachel to. What about this policeman—what was his name?"

"No," I said. "That isn't likely. We met almost no one. And Raleigh would have given them to me when I was down."

"What do you think I should do with it?"

I did not answer her right away. The doll seemed to look at me as though it could see and think, as though there was purpose behind those glass eyes.

"I don't think you should give it to Rachel," I said finally. I paused. "I think . . . I think it might be best to burn it."

Susan looked at me, shocked.

"Burn it? I don't understand. It's quite a lovely doll. An antique. And possibly quite valuable. Why on earth should I burn it?"

"I can't explain. I'm not even sure myself. But I

don't think you should give it to Rachel. At least not until . . ." I hesitated. "Not until we know for sure who sent it."

Susan nodded. I could see she did not understand. But tonight I was excused, tonight even my wildest behavior would be put down to the strain of the inquest.

"I think I'll go to bed," I said. "I'm overwrought."

"Yes. You're not yourself. I'll come up with you, I have to be up early in the morning."

We climbed the stairs together, going quietly to avoid waking Rachel. At the door of my room, I turned to say good night.

"Peter, if it would help . . ." I saw her looking at me anxiously. "Tim's away, he needn't know. . . ." Her voice trailed away.

"You're offering to sleep with me?"

She nodded.

"If it would help. If it would comfort you."

I could not answer straightaway. It had been a long time since our brief affair.

"Yes," I said. "It would comfort me. But better not. I don't think you'd like yourself very much in the morning. You're happy with Tim. Don't spoil it. Not for me."

"You're sure?"

"No, of course I'm not sure. Go to bed. We could both do with some sleep."

She smiled and kissed me on the cheek. I felt her burning there for a long time afterward.

It must have been around three or four o'clock when a noise woke me. I pulled myself up on the pillow and strained to see in the darkness. The room was very cold. I sensed more than saw that the door was open.

Had Susan decided to comfort me after all? I reached out my hand and switched on the light.

Rachel was standing in the doorway. She was wearing her red pajamas and the huge Mickey Mouse slippers Tim had bought her for Christmas. Her hair was tousled, and her eyes were full of sleep. In her arms she cradled the doll that had been posted to her.

"Why did you hide Mr. Belkins?" she asked.

I looked at her, not knowing what to do or say.

"I found him downstairs," she said. "I had a dream and I found him when I woke up. Nobody told me he was here."

"He isn't yours," I said. "He belongs to another little girl. I have to give him to her tomorrow."

She shook her head and clutched the doll more tightly.

"Oh, yes, he is mine. Mr. Belkins has always been mine."

"Why do you call him that?" I asked. "I didn't think he had a name."

She nodded emphatically.

"Yes, he does have a name. He's Mr. Belkins. I called him that before, and now I'm calling him that again."

"Before?" It was a question I knew I should not have asked.

"He was my doll before," she said. "When I lived at Petherick with Mummy and Aunt Agnes."

CHAPTER 17

By THE NEXT morning, Rachel seemed to have forgotten all about the doll or her appearance in my room. I had taken her back to bed and, once she was sleeping, removed Mr. Belkins from the room. Downstairs, I had crushed the doll's porcelain head and body and burned its clothes. The smell had lingered in the living room for a long time afterward.

Susan had finished her series and was free to look after Rachel again. I said I planned to go to York for the day, to visit some bookshops. Before I left, Susan took me aside.

"Peter, what happened to the doll?"

"I destroyed it."

She looked shocked.

"That was going a bit far, wasn't it?"

"Trust me, Susan. I did the right thing. It's for Rachel's good, for her safety. You know how important that is to me. I want you to keep a close eye on her while I'm away."

"Peter, you're frightening me. What is it? What's going on?"

I hesitated for a moment.

"I can't tell you now," I said, "really I can't. But you must promise not to let her out of your sight."

I know Susan wanted to ask me more, but there was nothing I could tell her. I kissed Rachel good-bye and took a cab to King's Cross.

Richard Adderstone lived in Helmsley, a pretty town in the Hambleton Hills, near Rievaulx Abbey. I hired a car in York and was in Helmsley shortly after two o'clock. I had not telephoned beforehand, fearing that Adderstone might prefer not to see a visitor who wanted to talk about Petherick House. It meant taking the risk of not finding him at home when I called, but the advantage of surprise that it gave me was too valuable to lose.

In the Black Swan they directed me to a Georgian house just off the market square. On a low metal gate the name of the house had been written in wrought-iron letters: St. Ives. I knew I had come to the right place.

A young woman answered the door. She was pretty, with long blond hair tied loosely at the back. I guessed her to be around twenty-five. She wore riding breeches and a tight-fitting cashmere jumper. I had not expected anyone so lovely to come to the door, and it quite destroyed the confidence I had been building up for the visit.

"Excuse me," I said. "I . . . I'm looking for a Mr. Adderstone. Richard Adderstone. This is his house, isn't it?"

She looked at me uncertainly. I could read the look on her face perfectly easily: a stranger meant someone from outside Helmsley, and outsiders would usually write or phone beforehand.

"I'm sorry, Mister . . ."

"Clare. Peter Clare. I've come up from London in the hope of finding him at home. It's not inconvenient, I trust?"

"Well, it could be. Richard Adderstone is my father. He . . . He hasn't been very well lately, and the doctor advises few visitors. Friends from the town call in from time to time. But you say you've come all the way from London?"

I nodded.

"It's really quite important," I said. "I'm sorry, I know I should have telephoned first. It's just that . . ." My voice trailed away. What excuse could I have offered, after all?

"Well . . ." She knew she could hardly send me away. "Perhaps you'd better come in. Will my father know who you are? I don't think I've heard him mention your name."

As she spoke she stood aside to let me into the hall. It was a spacious, uncluttered vestibule, with plenty of light entering it through windows by the door and along the stairwell onto which it led. Mirrors reflected the light in groups of three. Across one wall hung a reproduction of a medieval tapestry—one of the Dame à la Licorne series from Cluny.

"No," I said, replying to her question. "He will not have heard of me. I've come . . . perhaps you could tell him that I'd like to speak about a house he owns down in Cornwall."

She looked sharply at me.

"Petherick?"

I hesitated.

"Yes. Yes, that's it."

"Oh, it's not for sale, I'm afraid. I wish it were, but

there's some stupid clause in the deeds or something. It has to stay in the family."

"No, you misunderstand. I don't want to buy it. But there are some questions I'd like to ask about it."

"What sort of questions? Are you a local historian?"

I shook my head.

"No. No, I'm a writer."

"Really? What did you say your name was?"

"Peter Clare."

Her eyes opened wide.

"Not *the* Peter Clare? I've read a couple of your books, you know. They're up in my room. *The Egyptian House*, that was the first, and then *Notebooks from Mars*. I've got a copy of the one you wrote a few years ago—what's it called?—*The German Shoemaker*."

"Austrian," I said. "*The Austrian Shoemaker*." I smiled. It was rare for me to meet anyone who had heard my name, let alone read one of my books.

"That's right. I haven't had time to read it yet. But I promise I'll start tonight."

"What about the early ones? *Day of Wrath*, for instance?"

She shook her head, a little troubled.

"No, I . . . I don't think I'd like to read those. Because of . . ."

I knew what she meant. I had written in those books about my daughter, Catherine, and her death, about my grief. Some people found them hard to read.

An awkward silence fell. I moved to retrieve the brief rapport we had achieved.

"You'll enjoy *The Austrian Shoemaker*," I said.

We talked for a little longer, and she made me promise to sign her copies before I left. The ice had been broken. I breathed a silent thank you to whatever saint or deity it is who looks after authors.

"I still don't really understand why you want to

speak to Father about Petherick House," she said. "It's a horrid place. I only went there once, and I was glad to leave. I wouldn't spend a night there if they paid me to. I'm glad you aren't thinking of buying it."

"I stayed there this summer," I said. "It was . . ." I hesitated. "I thought of writing some stories, maybe a novel based on it. But I need to know a bit more about its history."

She looked at me steadily for several moments. Had she guessed that I was lying? I wondered how much she really knew about the house.

"Father mentioned that someone had rented the house. He wasn't very happy about it, you know. It was never his intention to let it out." She let her eyes rest on me, as though about to say more, then seemed to think better of it.

"Why don't you wait here?" she said. "My father's upstairs in his bedroom. I'll go up and tell him you're here. He won't have heard of you. He's not very fond of modern literature, I'm afraid, but I'll do my best to fill him in. I'm sure he'll see you."

As she turned to go up the stairs I called after her.

"I'm sorry," I said, "but I didn't get your name."

She smiled sweetly.

"Susannah," she said. "Susannah Adderstone."

He greeted me with great politeness, showing me to a chair next his. The bedroom was large and comfortable, filled with the bits and pieces needed to make an invalid comfortable. He was dressed in a silk dressing gown, beneath which he wore a striped shirt and bow tie. His silver hair was immaculately combed, his cheeks clean-shaven. An ivory-handled stick leaned against the side of his armchair. I thought he must be in his early sixties.

"My daughter tells me you are a famous writer, Mr. Clare."

I shook my head.

"Not famous. I've published a few books that have been well received. But I haven't written much in years. The public are fickle. And literary editors even more so."

"I have no doubt. My own contact with such matters is strictly limited. I once published a collection of essays on Cellini. It sold a few copies."

He paused and scrutinized me more closely. I sensed that he was uneasy about something. Even as he spoke he assiduously avoided meeting my eyes.

"Susannah tells me you have some questions to ask about Petherick House. I understand you are the gentleman who was conned by an unscrupulous young clerk at my solicitor's this summer."

I nodded.

"I see," he said, drawing the words out. I noticed that his hands moved nervously on his lap. The backs of them were mottled, with dark veins. "That really should never have been allowed to happen. I had given the most strict instructions. The house was never to be lived in under any circumstances. The terms of my aunt's will required me to keep it furnished and in good repair, but that is all."

He paused.

"The police were here," he said. "I had nothing to tell them. They did not explain the reason for their interest in the house. I thought it was simply because of the fraud. But perhaps there was something more."

I nodded. He did not look surprised.

"My daughter tells me you wish to write about the house in one of your books."

"Not exactly," I said. "I am less interested in the house than in what . . . inhabits it."

He brought his hands together like crabs, locking the fingers as though to keep them still.

"Inhabits . . . ?"

"Mr. Adderstone, I think you know very well what I mean."

He seemed about to deny this, but, on the verge of speaking, closed his eyes. Thus he remained for upward of a minute. When he opened his eyes again, his expression had changed to one blended of fear and pity.

"Perhaps," he said, "you would care to tell me what happened to you there."

I told him everything. The whole story from start to finish, from our arrival and Sarah's disappearance, right through to the inquest. He listened to me in silence, like someone who has heard a tale repeated many times and yet continues to hang on every word in the hope that it may have changed. His eyes remained firmly fixed on a spot on the wall opposite.

When I came to a halt, he said nothing for a long time. His vision seemed fixed elsewhere, not in the room at all. I let the silence grow until it filled every corner. It was a deep silence. I could hear my own breath in it. Finally, he lifted his sad eyes to me.

"It is worse than I feared." He hesitated. I saw his eyes wander to a painting on the wall. I followed his gaze. The painting was of a very young woman in a white dress.

"That is my first wife, Bryony," he said. "Did you know that she also disappeared at Petherick House?"

"Yes," I said. "Mr. Pentreath mentioned it."

"We had gone there shortly after our honeymoon. I thought . . . I foolishly thought that her presence there might drive out whatever evil remained. I even believed we could make a home there. But she hated it from the moment she set foot inside. We both thought the feeling would pass, but it grew stronger each day we stayed. Then, just as we had made our minds up to leave, she vanished. I never set eyes on her again."

For a moment he was lost in memory. Then his eyes found mine again and he resumed.

"I thought that perhaps it had ended by now. That you would have seen nothing and heard nothing. But I see that I was wrong."

There was a long pause. I said nothing.

"You say you were there two months?"

"It became quiet," I said. "Not long after Sarah's . . . disappearance." I was not sure what word to use. "Death" still seemed too final.

"You mean her 'vanishment.'"

"I'm sorry?"

"That is what my aunt called it. Whenever she spoke of her sister. Susannah." He paused. A cloud of pain seemed to cross his eyes. "My daughter is named after her," he went on. "I gave her the name in an act of defiance. And I pray I do not live to regret it."

He took a small handkerchief from his pocket and wiped his brow.

"Is there anything I can get you?" I asked.

He shook his head.

"I shall be all right."

There was a short pause.

"You said Agnes referred to her sister's disappearance as a 'vanishment.' Did she mean anything particular by that?"

"I think," he said, "that your wife's was a true vanishment. Like my Bryony's. It's an old term, one that the local people used to use. You don't hear it nowadays. I don't expect it was heard much in my aunt's day either. It referred to cases of mysterious disappearance, when a child or a young adult might go missing.

The farmers said that an evil spirit had come for them in the night, and that this spirit was keeping them under the earth. Well, that's all old wives' tales. And yet there may be some truth in them."

"Agnes thought that Susannah had been snatched away?"

He shook his head slowly.

"No. That was what she wanted people to think. She knew the locals, knew they were superstitious. The story of a vanishment kept tongues from wagging. No one asked too many questions about a thing like that. Not in those days. But my aunt knew better than that. She killed Susannah herself."

CHAPTER 18

"My aunt, Mr. Clare, was the most evil human being I have ever known. Believe me, I do not exaggerate. I did not know much of her as a child, but in the last year or two before she died, I visited her from time to time. I was a very young man then. When I was younger, I had been kept away from my aunt Agnes, but once I reached the age of twenty-one, I felt free to see anyone I wanted. She was really my great-aunt. My father was a grandson of Jeremiah Trevorrow's second wife by an earlier marriage. His father—my grandfather, that is—was brought up quite separately from the Trevorrows by his father's side of the family, the Adderstones.

"During those visits she began to tell me a little of her past. She had not really talked with anyone in half a lifetime, and now she had someone to whom she could unburden herself. She still lived then in Petherick House. It was where she died."

"But I thought she . . ."

He shook his head.

"She once tried to get away. The house in Truro had belonged to her father. He had once had business in the city that took him from home for days or weeks at a time. She kept the house, and now and then paid visits there. But she always went back to Petherick. Susannah would not let her leave."

"I don't understand."

The room in which we sat looked out over a quiet lane. Every so often there would be the sound of someone passing, or a car going through the market square. Then silence would fall again.

"Something happened in 1887," he said. "She told me some of this before she died. The rest I found out for myself. Until now, I have kept it all to myself. But I do not think I can withhold any of it from you. You have suffered enough already. You deserve to understand a little. It may set your mind at rest.

"It's important to go back a few years before Susannah's vanishment. Jeremiah Trevorrow had two daughters, each by a different wife. His first wife, Esther, died when Susannah was two. Jeremiah married Elizabeth-Jane Wilkes, the daughter of one of his tenants. She had been married once before, as I said, to my grandfather, George Adderstone. She and Jeremiah had a baby within the year. Four years separated the two girls. And more than just years.

"Susannah, the older girl, was, by all accounts, a charming child and a lovely young woman. I have a photograph of her. I'll show it to you later. It seems that she was always her father's pet. He had loved her mother desperately, and only married Elizabeth-Jane to provide for her nursing. Agnes he did not love. She was as pretty a child as Susannah, but for one thing— a birthmark had disfigured her. Whether because of that or not, she had a crabbed, sour personality. Perhaps such a disfigurement would not matter so much nowadays, but it was a severe affliction then. Her father's treatment of Agnes and her mother twisted her and made her the wounded, spiteful creature she became.

"This pattern was well established by the time the girls were in their teens. When Susannah was fifteen and Agnes still only eleven, Jeremiah's second wife died. By all accounts, Elizabeth-Jane Trevorrow had been a weak-willed woman. She had known of the rivalry between the two girls, of Agnes's growing hatred for her sister, and been either unwilling or unable to amend matters.

"With her death, the balance within the household grew even more unhealthy. Susannah attached herself more closely than ever to her father. She was a beautiful woman, and more than one man had shown an interest in her, but from the time of her stepmother's death, she vowed to devote herself solely to Jeremiah Trevorrow's well-being. He was a selfish man, and took keen advantage of her devotion. Agnes did the fetching and carrying, but Susannah got the credit for it. I don't think she ever meant her sister harm. Quite the contrary. As I say, she was good-natured and perfectly unselfish. But Agnes grew to resent her situation more and more.

"From the age of about sixteen, Agnes began to find consolation in the church. She was never, so she told me, a pious woman, but she was sick at heart and in need of a life outside Petherick House. In time she got a reputation for sanctity. Plain or blemished women often take that way out.

"And then, when she was seventeen, she had a proposal of marriage. A new vicar had come to Tredannack a year earlier, and his parishioners had been urging on him the need to find a wife. He chose Agnes Trevorrow. Her disfigurement was almost a mark of divine favor. She accepted, and plans were made for a wedding in the following year.

"It was a few months after that disaster struck. Susannah Trevorrow became pregnant. They tried to keep it in the family, but in a small place like that it was a hopeless undertaking. Within a short time the entire parish knew. There was a meeting between Agnes and her vicar. It was, of course, now out of the question for her to become his wife. It would have ruined him, and he was, it seems, an ambitious man.

"Well, Susannah had her baby in due course. She would never say who the father was, but from certain hints Agnes learned—or at least convinced herself—that her own father was responsible. From that time, her hatred for both her sister and her father turned to loathing mingled with a desire for revenge.

"The Trevorrows became even more reclusive than they had been. No one in Tredannack or St. Ives would receive them, nor did anyone visit them at Petherick House. The few servants they had abandoned them. The child, Catherine, took after her mother in looks and character. When she was almost three years old, Agnes discovered something that turned her mind completely. She found a copy of her father's will in a drawer. It declared Susannah to be Jeremiah Trevorrow's absolute heir. Petherick House, the house in Truro, and the lands 'round Tredannack were to be hers, while an annual allowance—a pittance—had been set aside for Agnes to live on. In the event of Susannah's death, the entire property, together with whatever capital was kept in the bank, would pass to Catherine, to be administered for her by trustees until she was twenty-five. Three deaths stood between Agnes and her freedom. And there was every reason to believe that Catherine might find a husband and have children of her own, to whom she would, naturally, leave her inheritance.

"Jeremiah Trevorrow died in February of 1887. The death certificate declares that he passed away from 'natural causes.' In fact, his daughter Agnes had been administering tiny doses of poison to him for several months. She let a little time go by after that before striking again. I think she had already some idea of the testimony she planned to give at the eventual inquest, to the effect that Susannah had been depressed following her father's death and so committed suicide. The months that elapsed between Jeremiah's death and Susannah's disappearance were intended to make the suicide more plausible."

Adderstone stopped speaking. I could see that something troubled him. Outside, silence had fallen over everything. A door opened and closed downstairs. I waited for him to resume.

"She was an old woman when she told me this," he said, "but it was as though it had happened the day before. Her memories would not give her peace. She did not tell me all at once, you understand. These were things she had kept locked away in herself for well over sixty years. They did not come into the light easily.

"She did not want to risk using poison again, for fear of exciting suspicion. Instead, she obtained a key to her sister's bedroom on the top floor. One evening, while Susannah was in the room, Agnes locked her inside. Catherine was with her. Agnes had already prepared two large bolts with padlocks to hold the door fast. She screwed them into place, ignoring the cries from inside. She had already nailed the window shut from outside.

"When the door was fastened to her satisfaction, she

went downstairs and made herself a meal. She remained downstairs for four weeks. Not once in all that time did she venture to her own bedroom. From time to time, she told me, she could hear her sister shouting. And more than once the sound of the child weeping, day after day, until silence returned. She told me that at such times she would sit with her hands over her ears, waiting for the crying or the shouting to subside.

"At the end of the fourth week, she went up to the room and unbarred the door."

He stopped speaking. I saw him shudder, as though he could see in his mind's eye the scene that had met Agnes Trevorrow's gaze when she opened that door. He had had many years to think about it, to dream about it.

"Susannah was still alive."

"Alive?"

"Please, let me go on. This is not easy for me. I say that Susannah was still alive. She had broken a pane of glass in the window and placed pots on the windowsill outside. That had allowed her to collect a little water when it rained. Luckily, it rains quite often in Cornwall. But having water had only served to prolong her agony. Without food of any kind, Susannah and her daughter had grown pitifully weak. In spite of her mother's attentions, the child had succumbed.

"When Agnes entered the room, she saw her sister squatting in the middle of the floor. She was quite mad, or seemed to be. The room had been ripped to shreds. Driven mad with thirst and hunger, Susannah had torn the bedclothes to pieces. She had stripped the paper from the walls. Her own clothes had been shredded. Agnes found her naked, staring through the window. There was . . ." I saw him choke, as though the words had thickened in his mouth. "There was a lot of blood."

"But how had she . . . ? How had she stayed alive on just water?"

"Surely," he said, looking up at me despairingly, "I do not have to spell it out to you? Please don't ask me to do that."

I felt sick. He could only mean one thing.

"What did Agnes do?" I asked.

"When she realized what had happened, she could not bear to go near her sister, not even to put an end to her sufferings. She closed the door and locked it again. Then she found the ladder and climbed to the bedroom window. Susannah was there, staring out at her. Agnes brought slats of wood and nailed them over the window, closing Susannah in. She left her there in the pitch darkness for another month. This time, when she opened the door, Susannah had been dead for some time. My aunt would not talk to me about what followed.

"All I know is that somehow she cleared the room. She disposed of Susannah's body that night, throwing her over the cliff. What Susannah had left of the child was buried somewhere in Petherick House. Agnes could never bring herself to speak to me of what happened after that. As you know, she continued to live at Petherick. I could never understand why. Not even now. I used to visit her there, you see, and I sensed that all was not well in the house. I would not myself have taken up residence there for anything. And yet somehow she continued to live there for sixty-six years, and I think that every day she relived what had happened all those years ago.

"I do not know what she heard or saw in that time, during those long winter nights when the house was in darkness and she had to face her ghosts alone. I shudder to think of it. But I believe it was with her own death that things took a turn for the worse. The ghosts of Susannah and her child are sad creatures. They can frighten, but I do not think they can do real harm.

"That is not the case with Agnes Trevorrow. She took her hatred and her bitterness and her anger to the grave with her. When I took Bryony to the house, it was because I believed the evil had departed with my aunt. But I was mistaken, fatally mistaken. The house had changed. Before, it had been disturbing. But then . . . then it held something positively evil."

He looked at me compassionately.

"It reached out for my wife. And now it has reached out for yours. I can only say that I am sorry."

He hesitated, as if steeling himself to ask something hard.

"Tell me," he said, "have you seen her since you were in Cornwall?"

"Seen whom?"

"My aunt. Agnes Trevorrow."

I told him of the glimpses I thought I had caught of a woman in London. And I mentioned the ring that had been sent to me, the doll that had come for Rachel. I said I thought it had somehow been Agnes Trevorrow's doing.

As I spoke I noticed that my host was growing more and more agitated.

"I'm sorry," I said. "I've been thoughtless. All this has upset you. Your daughter warned me you were ill."

"Please," he said. He was gasping now. "Over there . . . on the . . . bedside table. The . . . silver box."

I fetched it for him and watched as, with shaking hands, he removed a tiny pill and slipped it beneath his tongue. Within a few minutes he had calmed down. He closed the box with a snap and passed it back to me. I replaced it on the little table and remained standing, intending to leave.

"Mr. Clare," he said. "Please listen to me carefully. Go back as quickly as you can to London. Do not under any circumstances allow the child Rachel out of your sight. She is in grave danger, very grave danger. If my aunt—or the creature that has taken her shape—should appear at your friends' house, for the love of God do not let her inside. And see that your friends do not let her in. No matter what she says. Do you understand me? It is most important. For the child's sake."

I nodded. My hands were sweating.

"Now go," he said.

I shook his hand and turned to the door.

Downstairs, Susannah was waiting for me. She had books ready for me to sign.

"Thank you for letting me see him," I said as I scribbled my name on the title pages. "I'm sorry if I've tired him, but there was nothing I could do to prevent it. There were . . . things which had to be said."

I could sense her trying to read my face to extract some sign of what had passed between her father and myself.

"You seem pale," she said. "Have you and Father had a row?"

I shook my head.

"No. We talked, that's all. We talked about Petherick House."

"And Agnes Trevorrow? Did he tell you that the house and his aunt have always been taboo subjects in this family? I've no idea why. I wish someone would tell me what's so special about them. Some ghastly family secret, I suppose."

I looked at her steadily.

"I think it would be better if you left the matter closed."

The seriousness of my manner communicated itself to her, as I had intended it to. We looked at one another for several seconds, then she drew a deep breath.

"I'd better go up," she said. "He's not as well as he looks."

She showed me to the door. I gave her my card and she slipped it into a pocket. As I stepped outside she shook my hand.

"Did he tell you that I was named after Agnes's sister?" she asked.

"I had already guessed," I said. "When you told me your name." I paused. "He told me he has a photograph of Susannah. I think he meant to let me see it. Perhaps you could have a copy made and sent to me. I'll pay you for it, of course."

"I can show you now if you like."

She reached into the neck of her sweater and drew out a large gold locket on a chain.

"Here," she said. "This is her. This is Susannah Trevorrow."

She prized the locket open with a thumbnail. It was an old locket, chased with fine lines of silver. I bent forward to look at the photograph. As I did so I suddenly felt as though the whole world had stopped moving.

The photograph in the locket was a head-and-shoulders portrait of a young woman with her hair arranged in an old-fashioned style. I knew her face already, I had seen it a million times. It was my wife, Sarah.

CHAPTER 19

SARAH'S FUNERAL took place on a wet Monday afternoon the following week. All our old friends were there, many of them people I had not seen or heard from in years. We formed a distinct group from Sarah's family, who occupied one side of the chapel and one side of the grave, as though to signify some sort of perpetual enmity. I knew I would not see the Trevors again, yet I felt genuine sympathy for them and wanted to tell them how much Sarah had meant to me.

The cemetery was the indifferent municipal place I had expected it to be, but there were trees that gave it a softer, churchyard air. All through the burial, there was a crunching sound as people moved from foot to foot on the gravel paths. The sky was the color of slate. A bird moved quietly through it, circling above our heads again and again.

Raleigh was there, a little apart from the rest of us,

neither family nor friend. I spoke to him afterward. His condition had deteriorated even in the short interval since the inquest.

"I'm to go into hospital soon," he said. "Things are taking a turn for the worse."

I did not want to give him false reassurances. People had done that with me when Sarah first went missing. "She'll turn up, you'll see." He knew he was dying. Whatever I told him would make no difference.

"I went to see Adderstone," I said.

"And did he have anything to say?"

I told him all I knew. He was silent for a while. The other mourners had reached the gate and were getting into their cars. I could see faces turned in our direction. A light rain had started to fall across the graves. "She was Sarah's double," I said. "Susannah Trevorrow and Sarah were identical. I was shown her photograph." I paused. "I think it's Susannah you see in your dreams," I continued, "not Sarah."

"Does it make any difference?"

"Perhaps," I said. "I'm wondering whose body was found on Zawn Quoits." It made no difference that I had found Susannah Trevorrow's remains in her coffin. When nothing added up, what did reason matter?

"I can't swallow that," he said.

"A few months ago I would have swallowed none of this."

We walked in silence to the gate. As we reached it I looked back. Workmen had started to cover Sarah's coffin with wet soil. Just behind them, a figure in black was standing, watching me. The gravediggers seemed unaware of her.

She was holding a doll in her arms, holding it up so that I could see.

*   *   *

We drove straight back to London after a short reception at my in-laws' house. It had been a stilted affair punctuated by stony glances and hushed conversations. Rachel was waiting up for us. She had been looked after by a close friend, Jennifer, whom Tim had briefed about keeping the door closed to any strangers. He and I had talked about Agnes Trevorrow and the possibility that she might turn up in search of Rachel, and he had taken the matter seriously. Susan still knew nothing other than what I had told her.

Tim and Susan were both busy with work they had put to one side for the funeral. I volunteered to put Rachel to bed. She had already been bathed and dressed in her pajamas. I tucked her in and read her favorite story: *Six Dinner Sid*, the tale of an enterprising cat who manages to fit in daily meals at six different households in the same street until a sudden cough leads to repeated visits to the vet and exposure.

When the story was finished, I turned down the light and started for the door. Rachel called me back.

"Why did Mummy tell me Auntie Sarah was dead?" she asked.

"Because she is, dear. We were all at her funeral today."

Rachel shook her head.

"No," she said. "That can't be true."

I looked at her. Her small face was fixed in an expression of intense perplexity.

"Why do you think that?"

She looked at me almost as if she knew what was going through my head.

"Because she was here last night. In my room. She spoke to me. She said she wanted me to go with her."

I shivered. My back was to the door. I wanted to look around.

"Did she say where to?"

"Oh, yes. She said I was to go back with her to the house I was in before. She said we would go together. I asked if I could have a kitten. She said I could."

That night I dreamed the last dream. I reached the top story of the house. In front of me the door of Susannah's bedroom was half-open. I did not want to go inside, but I felt a force compelling me, pressing me forward until I was only inches from the doorway. There was someone inside. I could hear a sound of weeping, a child sobbing bitterly.

I stepped inside. An oil lamp was lit on the mantelpiece, filling the room with light and shadows. A small child in a long white dress was standing beside the bed, her back turned to me. I felt my hair stand on end as though a spider had walked over my skin. All the time I wanted to run, but I could not. The child started to turn. It felt as though cobwebs were touching my face. She began to turn, and I felt more frightened than I had ever felt in my life. She turned, and as she did so I woke with a start, snarling and yelping loudly enough to wake the entire household.

I reached out my hand to turn on the light. As I did so I realized with a stab of absolute dread that I was not in Tim and Susan's house. I was in my old bedroom in Petherick House. And there was something bumping in the next room.

I do not know how to explain what I have just written. Please try to understand. I was not asleep—I had just woken abruptly, and I was wide-awake. I was not dreaming. Somehow, I was fully conscious and fully aware of my surroundings. The room I was in was the bedroom in Petherick House, the one in which Sarah and I had slept. Nothing had changed since I had last been there. The sound of bumping continued without pause.

I lay for a long time, listening to the bumping noise and trying to reason with myself. I knew it was impossible for me to be where I was, but I could not doubt the evidence of my senses. The bumping would not stop. Cautiously, I sat up in the bed. I could see my shadow cast on the opposite wall. My heart was beating rapidly, quite out of time with the bumping next door.

I do not know how long I lay like that, sweating, shivering, unable to move a muscle. The bumping went on and on. In the end, I knew there was nothing for it. I could not just lie there, doing nothing, waiting for whatever was in the house to come for me. I pulled back the sheets and eased myself to the floor. A step at a time, I walked to the door. Holding my breath hard, I opened it. A woman was standing on the landing, watching me.

It must have been only seconds, but it seemed as though minutes passed before I realized that it was Susan. A moment later Tim appeared behind her. I looked around quickly. The room in which I was standing was my bedroom in their house.

"Peter, what's wrong? You look ghastly."

"I'm all . . . I'm all right."

"We heard you crying out," said Tim. "Did you have a nightmare?"

I nodded, finding words hard.

"Can I get you something? A drink maybe?"

I shook my head.

"No, I'm fine, really. I'm over it now. A bad dream, that's all. I hope I haven't woken Rachel."

"I'll look in on her," Susan said. "But are you sure you're all right, Peter? You don't look it. I think Tim's right, you should have a brandy or something."

"Really," I said, "I'm fine." I could still hear the bumping sound somewhere in my brain. Perhaps I was going mad after all. "It's the strain after the funeral and everything," I said. "But I'll be all right. I'll stay up for a bit, if you don't mind. I think a stiff drink might do me good after all."

To be honest, I was frightened to return to bed. I stayed in the kitchen all night, listening for sounds that did not come. When dawn came, I went back to bed and slept soundly for several hours. I had no more dreams that night. And when I woke, I was still in London.

CHAPTER

20

LATER THAT MORNING, I had coffee with Susan in the kitchen. Rachel had been left at the playgroup she sometimes attended. I noticed that Susan seemed awkward with me. There were long silences. Finally, I asked her what was wrong.

She took a long time to answer, sipping her coffee and putting the cup back on the table several times before she spoke.

"Tim told me everything last night," she began, as though pushing something ugly into the open. "About Sarah's disappearance. The Trevorrow woman." She shuddered and looked at me angrily. Her unbelief had been transformed overnight into harrowing fear. Whatever terrors her skepticism had been holding in check had woken up now and were walking openly through her mind.

"Why didn't you tell me? Why didn't you give me a chance to do something, to make up my own mind?

Jesus, anything could have happened to Rachel. That doll—she sent that, didn't she? That's why you burned it."

"I'm sorry . . . I . . ."

"Don't tell me about being sorry, because I don't want to know. I thought you loved Rachel, Peter, I thought you cared for her. Tim and I trusted you with her, we never questioned having you with her. But you actually came to live here, knowing all that had been going on. Are you completely mad?"

"I had no reason to think anything would happen here. And when they found Sarah's body . . . I thought it was over, Susie, I really thought it had ended."

"And has it?"

I hesitated.

"I . . . No, I don't think so. I don't understand what's going on, but I don't think she's done with me yet."

"And Rachel—has this woman done with her?"

"I don't think Rachel's involved. She—"

"Oh, for Christ's sake, Peter. You must think I'm stupid. These nightmares she's been having, the screaming fits, all that talk about not wanting to go back someplace she lived in before this. She told me herself about the doll, she said it had belonged to her in another life." Susan paused. She was shaking like a leaf. "She's the little girl, isn't she? She's come back in my daughter. That's the truth, isn't it?"

I said nothing.

"Well, you aren't going to deny it, are you?"

"No."

She looked at me hard. I could feel her anger.

"Do you know, Peter, I don't think it could have been worse if I'd come home and found you with your hand in her knickers."

"That isn't fair," I said. "You know it isn't. I've done

everything possible to protect Rachel. I destroyed the doll. I warned you against leaving Rachel alone. I kept a close eye on her when I was here. What more could I do? I'm as much out of my depth in this thing as you are."

"Nevertheless, you came here without thinking of the consequences." She let her gaze drift away. "Peter, I think you'd better leave. Go back to your own flat. This was only to be a limited stay anyway."

"All right. If that's what you'd like."

"Yes, it's what I'd like."

"I'm sorry, Susie. I don't mind going. I know I've stayed longer than I should have. I'll get my things now. Maybe you and Tim can come over for supper in a day or two and we can talk things over then."

I got up and went to the door.

"Peter."

Susan was still sitting at the table. I turned.

"I'm sorry, too," she said. "About Sarah. About whatever this thing is you've got yourself mixed up in. It's just that . . . I don't want anything to do with it. And I want to keep Rachel safe."

"I know you do. I want to see she's safe as well."

I did not tell her what Rachel had said to me the night before.

I saw little of Tim and Susan over the next few weeks, and Rachel only once. Time was heavy once more. The days passed slowly. Winter settled on the city and on me. There were no more dreams, or at least I did not wake remembering any. I do not think I dreamed at all. Sometimes I would wake at night, thinking there were voices in the flat, but when I looked, it was always empty.

With Sarah dead, I changed everything. I gave her

clothes to the Salvation Army, her jewelry to various friends. There were photographs of her everywhere: I put them in drawers and shut them away in the darkness. She was often in my thoughts, but I found it increasingly hard to see her face in my mind's eye. And if I ever did, it was not Sarah that I saw, but a sepia image of Susannah Trevorrow.

My writing went well, all things considered. I had embarked on another novel, my first in over three years. I wrote in the mornings and spent most afternoons in the library, reading, or pretending to read. From time to time I would look up if an attractive woman passed. The confusion I felt between occasional sexual desire and grief left me depressed and weary.

Once or twice I thought I caught a glimpse of a woman in a black dress, but when I looked more sharply, it was always someone else. Once I mistook an elderly priest in his black suit and hat for her. I began to reason that it had all been a terrible fantasy, brought on by stress when Sarah went missing. Then I thought of Richard Adderstone and the things he had told me. He had not told me everything. I was certain he had been holding something back. But he had said enough to convince anyone that none of what had happened had been a fantasy. And I knew that this was simply the calm before a coming storm.

In early November, a letter reached me from Raleigh. It had been posted from a hospital in Truro. His illness had progressed too far to admit of any possibility of cure, even had a powerful enough drug been available.

I lie here [he wrote] with scarcely the will to move. Writing is an intolerable burden. My children do not visit me. My ex-wife stays away. I am dying of loneliness.

In the mornings and late evenings I cough heavily, sputum and blood alike. There are fevers which leave me shaken and shivering in my bed. The nurses come and go, cheerful and efficient, but all of them know I am dying. Your wife is here most of the time now. They let her sit and watch by my bedside.

Before coming here, I discovered something I know you will find strange. The police officer in charge of the search for Susannah Trevorrow was a St. Ives man called Inspector Burrows. I wanted to know more of him. Perhaps he had left comments on the case. I tracked him down at last in a file in police archives. John Burrows died on the seventh of December 1887, only a few months after the Trevorrow inquest. He died of pulmonary tuberculosis, as I am about to die of it.

I had inquiries made in Tredannack, to see if anyone there might have sent the ring and doll to you. We found no suspects, but we did uncover something of interest. Your wife's was not the first disappearance in the region. You know about Adderstone's wife, of course. But for about thirty years, on and off, a number of women and children have vanished in and around Tredannack. The locals have a word for these disappearances. They call them vanishments. But they will not speak freely of them, or give details. The children are always girls aged four or thereabouts. And the women are always your wife's age or younger. The people of Tredannack live in a state of fear. They watch their wives and children constantly. Even the vicar is frightened and will not talk.

She was here last night, in the ward. It was after

midnight, I think, though I have lost track of time in here. She sat in a chair facing the bed, watching me. Not your wife, I do not mean her. The other one. Agnes.

Did I tell you that someone dug up Susannah Trevorrow's grave? It was the night before the inquest. Like you, I have begun to wonder whose body it was we found on Zawn Quoits. Perhaps your wife knows. If it is your wife who visits me here.

That was all he wrote. I wrote back telling him what he knew already, that I had opened Susannah Trevorrow's grave. He did not reply. A couple of weeks later I had a letter from the hospital. He had asked them to let me know when he died. A funeral had been arranged for the following week. It was winter, and the trees outside my study window were already bare.

I went to Raleigh's funeral. His ex-wife and children were there, and colleagues from the force. At least they did not bury him alone. I was the last to leave the churchyard. What did I hope to see? My dead wife come to sit by his grave? Susannah Trevorrow with her child, floating like spindrift across the headstones?

It must have been about a week afterward that Rachel had her first fit. I only learned of it a few days after it had happened, when I called on Tim and Susan late one evening on my way home from the pub. I had been drinking alone as usual. Somehow, I seemed to have been doing a lot of that since the inquest. Relations between Tim, Susan, and myself had recovered, though they were far from what they had once been. Susan still distrusted me and thought it dangerous to have me around her daughter. I had only seen Rachel twice in as many months.

When I asked about her, Susan glanced at Tim anxiously, as though she was unsure what I should be told.

"She had a fit a couple of days ago," said Tim.

"I don't understand. Do you mean epilepsy?"

He shook his head.

"They don't know. She had one of those screaming attacks during the night. When Susan went in, she found her in convulsions. She managed to calm her down eventually while I called the doctor. He had her taken straight into hospital for tests. Everything came back negative. We've no idea whether it will happen again, or when."

It did happen again, the following day. And two days after that. Each time a team of doctors ran tests on her, each time they came back empty-handed. She was given Carbamazepine, a common antiepileptic, which her doctor recommended taking several times per day. Two days after that, she had her worst seizure, in the course of which she bit her tongue badly, requiring stitches. Tim rang me the following morning.

"Susan doesn't know this," he said. "I was the first to go in while Susie was getting the medicine. Rachel was on the bed, writhing up and down. She was being flung all over the place like a rag doll. The lamp on the bedside table was knocked to the floor." He paused. "Rachel didn't touch it. I saw for myself. The lamp was picked up and hurled to the ground. There was something in that room besides Rachel."

"Can I see her?"

"Susan doesn't want you here. She thinks you're responsible for all this."

"You know that isn't true."

"No, Peter, I don't know that. You may have intended none of this to happen, but it is happening nonetheless. We're at our wits' end. It just can't go on like this."

"I'll think of something," I said. "I promise."

Two nights later I had a call from him.

"Peter, can you stay the night?"

"What's wrong?"

"Susie had to go off at short notice. *The Sunday Times* needs her to interview this German fascist leader the Home Office wants to deport. She didn't want to leave Rachel, but I insisted. Frankly, I thought it would do her good to get away. She's worn-out, Peter; she needs a break."

"And you want me over there?"

"I need someone to help. Jennifer said she'd come over, but she rang five minutes ago to say she can't make it after all."

"What if something happens?"

"It's already happening. I don't think your presence will make the slightest difference. And I'd like you to see it for yourself anyway. The attacks are getting worse."

"Shouldn't she be in hospital?"

"That's being considered. But for the moment we want her at home. Apart from the fits, she's perfectly all right."

I was there in twenty minutes. It was still early, and I spent over an hour playing with Rachel. As Tim had said, she seemed fine, except for some bruises, which he said she had received in the course of the fits. When she had been put to bed, Tim switched off the television and made us both drinks.

"She looks better than I feared," I said.

"Yes, she's bearing up well. But the attacks are having their effect. She gets less sleep than is good for her. Susan makes sure she has a nap in the day, but it's not the same."

"Don't the fits happen then?"

Tim shook his head.

"Just at night. She goes to sleep, wakes screaming, and then it starts. The medication only makes her drowsy the next day, otherwise it does nothing. It's starting to wear her out. If we don't find an answer soon . . ."

"Aren't the doctors doing anything?"

"She was given a brain scan last week. Nothing. Absolutely nothing."

"Have you thought of trying something else? A homeopath, a cranial osteopath— I don't know."

"We've talked about it. Yes, if the hospital doesn't get anywhere. But these attacks are so violent."

We drank and talked for a long time. It was like old times. Except for an unfamiliar tension between us. No, not quite unfamiliar, but stale, dredged up from a past we had both put behind us. Every so often Tim would glance at the ceiling, as though bracing himself for what might be about to come. But nothing happened. The house remained still. I looked at the clock. It was well after midnight.

"I think she's going to have a quiet night," said Tim. "Let's go to bed."

I slept in my old room. Tim had made hot water bottles for us both, and I luxuriated in the unaccustomed warmth of my bed. I soon fell asleep. I do not recall now if I dreamed or not. But at some point—it must have been about 3:00 A.M.—I remember struggling out of sleep to strange noises. Muffled screams were coming from Rachel's bedroom. A moment later they stopped, to be replaced almost at once by a quick, frenzied banging, then a sound of smashing glass.

I leapt out of bed and dashed into the corridor. Tim was already there, at the door of Rachel's room. He flung the door open and rushed in, switching on the light as he did so. I hurried after him.

The bedclothes had been torn back and hurled to the ground. Rachel lay on crumpled sheets, her back arched, her arms thrown out stiffly at her sides. The room was freezing cold. As I came through the door a row of books in the shelf to the left of the bed came flying out one by one, landing in a heap at the foot of the wall opposite. The light that hung from the center of the ceiling was spinning around and around like a flail.

Tim was at Rachel's side, trying to quiet her. The next moment she seemed to take off. Her body stiffened and jerked away from Tim. I looked on in horror as she was lifted, thrown onto the mattress, and lifted again, as though someone had her by the ankles and was shaking her. There was a loud explosion as the window burst into fragments, showering the curtains with glass. Toys were hurled with terrible force in all directions, sometimes striking Tim or myself. There was a ripping sound as the carpet pulled away from the tacks holding it to the floor. On the bed, Rachel was in convulsions, her entire body rippling as though an electrical current was being passed through it.

I rushed to the bedside to help Tim hold her down. The moment I touched her she went limp and fell to the bed. All the objects that had been flying through the air of the room fell to the ground. There was an intense silence. Rachel lay as though unconscious.

Suddenly, from nowhere in particular, we both

heard a voice. It was a woman's voice, the same voice I had heard months earlier in Petherick House.

"Catherine. Wait for me, Catherine."

The next moment Rachel opened her eyes.

"Mummy," she cried. "Where are you, Mummy?"

And then she looked at Tim and myself, realized where she was, and burst into tears.

CHAPTER

21

RACHEL SLEPT LATE while Tim and I both sat with her. When she finally awoke toward noon, she had forgotten everything about the night before. Tim had not called the doctor. After what he had seen, he no longer saw any point in fooling himself that medicine could be of the slightest help.

"How long is it going to continue?" he asked, again and again. I had no answer for him. But I thought I could begin to see my way toward one, however imperfectly. *When Susannah Trevorrow finds her daughter again* was what I thought, though I said nothing to Tim.

I went back home that afternoon. Susan would be returning before long, and Tim did not want her to find me there. A small package was waiting for me. It bore a Helmsley postmark. Inside I found a letter and a small clothbound book.

The letter was signed *Susannah Adderstone*. I read it quickly.

Dear Mr. Clare,

I hope you will forgive my writing like this. Father is very ill. The doctor says he may not have much longer to live. He does not say so, but it is since your visit that he has gone into this decline. I do not say this to blame you. But I thought you should know.

He wants me to send you the enclosed book. It's a sort of journal kept by my great-aunt, Agnes Trevorrow. He has asked me not to read it, and I have not done so. He says you will understand what is in it, and hopes it will be of some help to you.

He has told me about your tragedy. I confess that I do not understand in what way it concerns my family, other than through the coincidence of your having been living at Petherick House when your wife disappeared. But I am not stupid. I know Father has kept a great deal back from me. Perhaps when he is dead, someone will let me into his great secret. I think you know a lot about it.

There is something I must tell you, though I do not find it easy. After you left, I reread those of your novels I had in the house. I also ordered copies of the early stories from the little bookshop here. I have read them all now. Shall I tell Father what is in them, or shall you? You know what I mean, of course. I wonder how you live with yourself, knowing the things you have written.

There is another thing you should know. Since you were here, I have been plagued by dreams. They are all variants of the same dream. There is a young woman and a child and, somewhere out of sight, another person. The young woman is Susannah Trevorrow, I recognize her from the photograph I carry. She seems to want something from me. I cannot tell Father, it would upset him. Is there anything you know, anything you can tell me? It is terrible waking in the middle of winter with those sounds in my ears. You cannot guess the silence here and how terrible it is when broken.

Yours faithfully,

Susannah Adderstone

I knew what she meant about my early novels. Anyone who has read them will understand. It was cruel of her to remind me like that.

I was loath to touch the journal, knowing whose hand had written it. I left it on my desk all the rest of that day. At times, I was tempted to do with it what I had done to the doll she had sent to Rachel. But I needed to know all I could about her. What had been in her mind, what hopes, dreams, and fears she had had, what she had known about herself.

The following morning it was still lying there, as though waiting for me. I tried not to look at it, but it seemed to call me to itself, and in the end I succumbed. I began to read.

There were no dates, neither days of the week nor numbers of the years. Just thoughts set down at random over time. How long? I could not guess. A year, perhaps. And maybe much longer. Over sixty years.

Every night now, and some days without cease. It is worse when the wind is up. It seems to drive her to the house. Sometimes I hear her laughing; that is the worst of all. God forgive me, I could kill her again then.

Three nights in a row, then silence. There are times I think the silence is worse than anything. I sit waiting for it to change. And when it does, when she comes again, I wish it would return. But I will not give her what she wants, however much she sits and stares, however plaintively the child cries.

I was at the cliff last night. In the dark you can pretend there is no distance between yourself and the water. A step would set me free. Or imprison me here forever.

Sometimes I go from room to room in search of her; but she is never there, and I go out, slamming the doors behind me. And then I come here to bed and lie awake, going from room to room in my mind. And in my mind I go through the house again, slamming more doors.

Woken at 3:00 A.M. last night by her screaming. I will not go up. That is what she wants, but I will not go.

The Reverend Sowerby died yesterday. He leaves his wife and four children. The funeral takes place on Friday, but I am not expected. I spent yesterday in tears. She did not leave me once all night.

My week in Truro was quiet, but I could not stay. At Petherick, I can hate her, I can almost justify what I did. But in Truro, I am alone with my conscience, and it will not give me rest. In its way, it is the greater torment. She has Petherick House for her playground, but my conscience has the world.

I heard the child passing my room last night several times. Why can she not keep still?

I have thought of burying the child with her mother, but I do not think I have the strength. And it would give her what she wants, it would give her peace. She does not deserve peace, for I have had none, and all on her account. If I hold out long enough, I shall have beaten her, I shall have beaten all of them.

The sea was high last night. I could hear the waves pounding the cliff wall. She sat in her room and screamed, but I pretended I could not hear her. Will winter never end?

By the end I almost pitied her. Trapped with her ghosts in a house she could not sell, her already small income diminishing visibly each year, the thought of those long winter nights constantly in her mind. She had not been welcome in the village, no locals would come to work for her, the only help she had was a woman from St. Ives who came once a fortnight to do a little cleaning. Her solicitors told her she could sell the house in Truro for a reasonable sum, but she refused to sell, regarding it as her only bolt hole, cherishing the dream that one day she might after all break free of her past and go there to live.

I was about to put the packaging in which the journal had come into the bin when I noticed that there was another enclosure. Fishing inside, I drew out a small brown envelope, the sort sometimes used to hold cash for the bank. It contained three keys and a short note.

Dear Mr. Clare,
    I have asked my daughter to place these in the packet she is going to post to you. I think you will know what to do with them. I do not have the courage to tell Susannah all I know. But after I am

gone, the house will be hers. Perhaps you will find some way to warn her. I think it will be for the best to have the place destroyed. Destroyed and, if possible, cleansed in some way. Do as you think best.

Richard Adderstone

I took the keys one at a time and laid them on my desk. I recognized them without prompting. They were the keys to Petherick House.

CHAPTER 22

THE WEATHER GREW steadily worse. There were fierce storms several nights in a row. Snow fell in Scotland and started to come south. In Cornwall, high seas rose over the walls of the harbors and sank fishing boats.

Rachel's condition grew worse. She was taken on a round of specialists, all of whom professed themselves perplexed. New drugs were tried, none to the least avail. The strain of the fits and loss of sleep was showing on her. She had lost weight, showed a perpetual pallor, and was growing sulky and irritable. Tim and Susan were frightened and desperate. I knew what had to be done, but I could not do it. Not yet, not while they were there. Susan would have stopped me, and that would have been the end for all of us. I bided my time. Every day I wrote three thousand words.

*　　　*　　　*

I heard of the accident while having lunch on the tenth of December. The radio was on in the background. It was during the final item on the news bulletin that I heard Tim and Susan's names mentioned.

"A couple were seriously injured today when their car overturned on the A40 between Oxford and Wheatley. No other vehicles were involved in the accident, which took place shortly after ten o'clock this morning. The car, a Ford Sierra, left the roadway without warning and overturned in a field, trapping the occupants. The names of the driver and passengers have now been released. They are Tim and Susan Wigram and their four-year-old daughter, Rachel, who was traveling in the rear. Mr. and Mrs. Wigram have been taken to the Radcliffe Infirmary, where they are in intensive care. Their daughter, who escaped unhurt, is also at the infirmary."

I drove straight to Oxford. By the time I got there, Tim had come out of intensive care and was under observation in a separate room. He had been badly smashed up. His bed was surrounded by a battery of machines, and he was hooked up to a battery of drips and feeds. Susan was in a coma. They told me Tim was still too ill to receive visitors, but they let me in to see Rachel.

She was being looked after by a nurse in a room off the main children's ward. When I came in, she burst into tears and clung to me tightly. When she was able to speak, I asked her what had happened.

"We were at the hospital," she said. "To see another doctor. I didn't like him. He was rough. And he had cold hands."

"What hospital was this, Rachel?"

"I don't know."

"Was it this one?"

"Maybe. I don't remember."

"And then you had a crash?"

"We were going home. A lady stepped into the road."

"And your daddy swerved the car?"

"I think so."

She fell quiet. Her normally bright expression was clouded and anxious.

"Will my mummy and daddy be all right?" she asked.

"Yes, of course they will. The doctors will take care of them."

"I don't like doctors," she said.

"These are nice doctors. They're going to help your mummy and daddy get well."

She looked at me as though she did not believe me.

"I don't want anything bad to happen."

"Why should anything bad happen?"

"Like before," she said. "When I lived in Petherick House."

I hesitated. Was it fair to press her when she was already under such strain? But I thought it was better to know.

"Do you know what happened then?" I asked.

She shook her head.

"I don't remember. But I know something bad did happen. Sometimes I dream about it. But later I forget again."

A policeman came soon after that. He had been directed to speak to me. I was able to give him what little information I had about Tim's parents. Susan's family had gone to live in Florida about eight years earlier. The policeman said he would make inquiries.

"Did you find the woman?" I asked.

"What woman, sir?"

"Rachel said that a woman stepped out in front of the car. That's why Tim swerved. It sent him off the road."

The policeman looked puzzled.

"I was at the scene of the accident, sir. There was no sign of anyone. But thanks anyway. I'll make inquiries."

"What about Rachel?" I asked. "What's to be done with her?"

"The little girl? I couldn't really say, sir. It's up to the social-work team here in the hospital. But I daresay the grandparents will just take her home with them."

"Christ!" I said. "I completely forgot. Tim's parents won't be at home. They go to Spain every winter. There's some tourist company that gives them pensioner rates. They spend two or three months."

"I see. Any idea where, sir?"

"I'm not sure. Tim will know. Torremolinos, Benidorm—one of those ghastly places."

He looked accusingly at me.

"Can't think what you mean, sir. That's where I spend my own hols. Benidorm. The wife and I have been going there for years. Lovely place. It shouldn't be too hard to track down the Wigrams there."

"Would they let me take the child? She knows me. Far better than some social worker."

"Wouldn't know, sir. If the father's conscious, they might ask him."

"All right. Thank you."

"Thank you, sir. We'll be in touch if there's anything more we need."

They let me in to see Tim an hour later.

"I can only give you five minutes. He's quite heavily sedated. There's been a lot of internal damage."

"But he will recover?"

The doctor was Pakistani. He had a quietly harassed look. The beeper sticking out of his pocket made him temporary to everyone and everything.

"In time, more or less. He may not be very mobile. It's far too early to tell the real extent of the damage. He still has to face quite a lot of surgery."

"And Susan?"

"His wife? I don't know. You'll have to speak to Dr. Shah. But I think he's gone off duty now. Sister will tell you something, I'm sure."

Tim was groggy, hovering between pain and sedation. He recognized me. I stood, looking down on him. All around us the humming of machinery dimmed the silence.

"Is . . . Susan all right?" was his first question. His voice was weak and hesitant.

"Yes," I said. "She's in another ward. She's fine."

"And Rachel? They . . . told me she wasn't hurt."

"That's right. She's in the children's ward, but it's only to keep an eye on her. She wasn't even scratched."

"Thank God."

He closed his eyes. I thought he might pass out on me.

"It was her," he whispered. I bent down to hear him better. "Susannah Trevorrow."

"I don't understand."

He opened his eyes. Almost the only light came from the machinery.

"She stepped out . . . in front of the car. A little bit ahead. I . . . thought it was Sarah, then I . . . remembered what you said. About them looking alike. She was just . . . standing there, facing the car. I knew I couldn't stop. So I . . . pulled the wheel. We were . . . going quite fast. Next thing I knew . . . I was in this place."

"Tim, you must have—"

"I know what I saw, Peter."

I did not answer. A nurse put her head around the door and indicated that my time was up.

"Tim, something has to be done about Rachel. I'd like to take her home. She can stay with me until you're both out."

He blinked and made a slight gesture with his head to signify assent.

"Yes," he said. "No one else will . . . understand. Jenny next door has the key to the house. You can get . . . Rachel's things."

The nurse came in and I left.

"He wants me to take care of his daughter," I said. "Can you fix things with the authorities?"

"I'll have a quick word with him."

When she came out, she said she thought it would be all right.

"You'll have to see someone on the social-work team. I'll show you the way to their office—there's usually someone there at this time. I'll ring them myself and tell them the father's given his consent."

The formalities did not take long to complete. I sensed that the social worker who spoke with me was only too glad I was willing to take Rachel off their hands. I filled in several forms, and when I left the office, Rachel was officially in my custody until Tim's parents could be tracked down.

I wanted to see Susan before leaving.

"Wait here," I told Rachel. "I just want to ask the doctor something."

A nurse directed me to the intensive-care unit where Susan was being kept.

"Is Dr. Shah still on duty?" I asked the sister.

"He went off a couple of hours ago. Can I help?"

"I just wanted to know if I could see Mrs. Wigram.

She was in an accident this morning. I'm looking after her daughter, and I'd like to be able to tell her I've seen her."

The sister bit her lip.

"Didn't they tell you?"

"Tell me what?"

"They should have told you. You say you were with her daughter? Are you a relative?"

"No. Look, what should they have told me? I'm a close friend. I'm taking care of Susan's daughter."

"Mrs. Wigram died an hour ago."

She brought a young doctor to speak to me. Her name was Ross. She told me she had been with Susan when she died.

"Did she come out of the coma?" I asked.

"Only briefly. A minute or two at the most."

"Did she say anything?"

She looked faintly troubled.

"She was . . . when she came out of the coma, she was shouting. I had to calm her down. Then she turned to me and said, 'It's starting all over again.' That's all. She repeated it several times. She died about a minute after that. I'm sorry."

We drove back to London in the dark. The highway was awash with cars and their lights. I did not tell Rachel of her mother's death; I tried to maintain a semblance of normality. Over and over again I imagined the figure of Susannah Trevorrow stepping in front of Tim's car, the car swerving, skidding, plowing into the empty field, overturning like a turtle, time after time. Why? What had she wanted? I looked at Rachel and wondered if this was what Susannah had wanted to achieve: her daughter returned and sitting here in the car with me. With me at last.

CHAPTER 23

I DROVE SLOWLY in the inside lane, half expecting to see a woman dash into my path, a white figure in the long beams of my headlights. It terrified me to think that Rachel might go into one of her fits in the car. If that happened, what on earth could I do? If I had enough warning, perhaps I could pull over onto the hard shoulder and sit it out there. But what if that was not all? What if something started happening to the car, just as I had seen happen to Rachel's room? She sat beside me, staring through the windshield. I wondered what she saw out there in the dark.

That night she slept soundly, and in the morning seemed more rested than she had done the day before. Sleep had restored a little of the color to her cheeks. She ate a large breakfast, and we talked about the things we planned to do that day.

I rang the Radcliffe, but all they could tell me was

that Tim had gone into surgery at nine o'clock and that he was not expected out until midafternoon. It was going to be a long operation. Had he been told of his wife's death? No, that would have to wait until he was much stronger.

I took Rachel over to her house in order to pick up some clothes and a few treasured possessions. Jenny—Tim and Sue's next-door neighbor—remembered me and came in to talk. She had already heard about the accident. I told her privately that Susan was dead, but that Rachel was not to know. She seemed genuinely grief-stricken and found it hard to control herself when we went to fetch Rachel from the garden.

"Can you look after her yourself?" she asked. "Wouldn't she be better off with a couple? Phil and I could take care of her for a while."

"Thanks for offering," I said, "but Tim wanted me to do it. I'd like to give it a try. I had a little girl of my own once. Of course, it would have been easier if . . ." I paused. "Did Susan tell you that my wife died?"

She nodded.

"I'm sorry. This is a bad time for you."

"Yes."

"Do you know about these attacks Rachel's been having?"

"Tim's told me all about them. I was there when she had one not long ago. I'll cope."

"They see Dr. Ronson in the High Street. Let me give you his number."

"It's okay," I said. "I can get it from the phone book. I'll be in touch if I need anything."

She had a fit at midnight, and another three hours later. Each time, the bed lifted from the floor. The temperature in the room sank below zero in a matter of seconds and stayed there until the fit had passed. This time I could hear voices, indistinct, as though relayed from a great distance.

Afterward, I went to my desk and took out the bunch of keys Richard Adderstone had sent me. I slipped them into my pocket.

I had started rereading my early novels.

The next day Tim was back in the operating room when I rang. Something had gone wrong with the operation the day before, and they had to correct it while there was still time. I hung up.

A moment later I picked up the receiver and punched in a second number. The phone rang for over a minute, but I hung on. Finally, someone answered.

"Hello," I said. "Is that Susannah?"

"Yes, speaking."

"Susannah, this is Peter Clare. I'm sorry to disturb you."

"No, that's all right. How can I help you?"

"Is your father well enough to speak to me?"

There was a brief silence.

"No, I don't think that's a good idea, Mr. Clare."

"It's important. There's something I need to know."

"Nevertheless. If you like, I'll ask him for you. Provided it's not something that's likely to distress him further."

"I just want him to tell me whether there was ever any extensive building work done inside Petherick House since it came into his possession."

"I don't think it would be a good idea to ask him that. Or anything else connected to that place. He gets very agitated."

"It is important. A child's life may be at stake."

She paused.

"I can ask the solicitors in St. Ives. They would know. They handled all that sort of thing."

"Yes, if you would. Thank you."

Another silence.

"Are you writing another novel, Mr. Clare?"

The question took me by surprise.

"Yes. Why do you ask?"

"Just curious," she said. "Is it to be like your previous ones?"

"Not much," I said.

"I'll ring the solicitors now. Give me your number and I'll ring you back."

She rang about an hour later. No major alterations had been done at Petherick House since Agnes Trevorrow's day. There had been some trivial redecoration inside, and regular pointing, reslating, and reguttering on the exterior.

Rachel was growing fretful.

"I want to see my mummy," she said. "And my daddy. Why won't you take me to see them?"

"I will as soon as I can, love. But they're both still in hospital, and we can't visit them until the doctor says so. Your daddy has had an operation, and we have to let him get a bit better before we can see him."

"Did they open him up?"

"Only a little."

"Did it hurt?"

I shook my head and tried to laugh.

"Of course not. They put you to sleep."

"I wouldn't like that."

"Having an operation?"

"Being put to sleep. I don't like to be asleep."

"Why not?"

But she clammed up and went off in search of Simpson, her favorite teddy bear.

I brought her bed into my room that night. She was asleep long before I came up. I lay awake for a long time, watching her, then fell asleep myself. Something woke me around three o'clock. The night-light by Rachel's bed was still lit. Standing quietly over her bed was a figure, barely visible. I made a movement, and the figure started, looking around. It was Susannah Trevorrow. I thought for a moment it might be Sarah, but the hair and clothes were different. She looked at me with such pain in her eyes. The next moment she was gone.

Rachel went on sleeping until dawn. From time to time a dream would send her into starts and twitches, but she never woke.

I rang the hospital first thing. They told me Tim had died in the night.

CHAPTER 24

THE ROAD TO CORNWALL had never seemed so open or
so desolate. Not in all the summers of my childhood
had I gone down it with such a heavy heart. The con-
voys of July and August had long since vanished. On
either side the fields were flat and sere; frost covered
them with a slick white skin. Here and there sheep
stood on the uncovered hillsides with their backs
against the wind. Above our heads, the sky floated
naked like the belly of a vast shambling beast.

Rachel sat in the front beside me, watching out for
the chimneys of tin mines, which had started to
appear above the fields. I had not told her that her
parents were dead. I thought that perhaps I might
never tell her. We could go on like this indefinitely,
Rachel and I. We could travel the world together and
never speak once of death.

I think she guessed where we were headed, though
I did not tell her that either. When we set off, I just

said we were going for a little holiday. I had no firm idea in my mind, other than that we had to get back to Petherick House. They were waiting for us. We had to go to them.

We passed through Tredannack quickly, almost furtively. The children were still in school, their mothers at home baking bread or watching television like Margaret Trebarvah. I understood Margaret and her fears now. Ted Bickleigh had been wrong. The police never would find the little body they sought.

The village had a lost, deserted air. No one was in the main street, not even a cat or dog. The cold marine air seemed to sit on the roofs and pavements with the weight of the sea itself.

The dark, familiar road. The sound of tires aching on the hard ground. Glimpses of sudden water shut in again by thin-branched trees and the hedges of my own disquiet. The dark-edged pale water that had swallowed Susannah Trevorrow, and my wife, and God knows how many others. If I caress you, I thought, will you give up your secrets? But how do you do that, how do you caress the sea?

The house was waiting for us, and behind it the sound of water crashing ashore. Rachel, who had been asleep, opened her eyes as we slowed and stopped at the gate. She turned as I drew up the hand brake and loosened my belt.

"We're here," she said.

"Yes, darling," I said. "Home again."

"I don't want to go. I'm frightened."

"What are you frightened of?"

"That something bad will happen, like before."

"Can you remember, Rachel?" I asked gently. "Can you remember what happened before?"

She did not speak at once. Something clouded her eyes. A shadow, something hinted at, that I could not find a name for.

Slowly she shook her little head from side to side.

"Something bad happened." The words were being dragged out of her, being dragged out of that other little girl who had died almost one hundred years ago. "I was called Catherine. I had a doll called Mr. Belkins and a kitten called Toby. Somebody hurt me. I was very cold. I was hungry."

"Who hurt you?" I asked. "Was it your aunt Agnes? Did she hurt you, darling?"

She shook her head. The questions were troubling her.

"I can't remember," she said. "I can't remember. Don't make me. I don't want to." She was on the verge of tears. I wondered what had made me bring her here.

"It's all right," I said, reaching for her. "Nobody's going to hurt you. Not this time."

She was hard to reassure.

"Will my mummy and daddy be coming here?" she asked.

"No," I said, holding my voice steady. "Not here. They're still in hospital. They have to stay a little longer."

She sank back into silence, into that little pool of loneliness only children know. How could I tell her that Tim and Susan could not come here because they were dead, that she would never see them again?

But then, on second thought, what did I know?

It felt like a real homecoming. Petherick House was mine again. For a moment I imagined living here for the rest of my life, writing book after brilliant book to the sound of the sea rattling. Getting out of the car, I shivered in the cold salt wind. Beyond, where the sea lay, thick clouds were piling up on the horizon.

We went inside. How still the house was. I switched on the light and headed straight for the meter beneath the stairs. Prudently, I had brought a bag of pound coins with me, and now I proceeded to stuff the meter with as many as would fit.

When I turned back to speak to Rachel, I saw her standing just inside the front door, staring up at the staircase. Her eyes were large and frightened. I could feel my heart begin to beat faster. Was it already starting? I joined her, taking her hand in mine.

"Can you see something?" I asked, following the direction of her gaze. The memory of my dreams came flooding back. But now I was here in the flesh, and the room of all my fears was there, unchanged, unchanging, at the top of the stairs. I only had to climb.

Rachel shook her head.

"No," she said. "Just the stairs. But I remember . . ." Her voice trailed away. I waited, but she did not go on.

"Are you hungry?" I asked. We had only eaten a snack on the way down, in a service station off the A30.

"Yes."

"Well, let's get our things out of the car, then we can cook something."

I put my bag in the room where I had slept before. Rachel wanted to sleep there with me. We found a small bed in another room and moved it to mine. When everything was settled, we went downstairs to the kitchen.

I remembered sitting there with Sarah on the night of our arrival, her nervousness, that moment when she told me she did not like Petherick House and that she wanted to leave. If I had listened to her, surely none of this would have happened. And yet I could not escape a terrible sense that everything that had taken place had been fated from the start. Sarah's resemblance to Susannah Trevorrow and Rachel's hazy memories of an earlier life as Susannah's child had not been coincidences. Something or someone had led me to Petherick House in the first place, and that same force had drawn me back again.

Thinking of Sarah made me jittery. The house had been quiet all through the second part of my stay in the summer, as though Sarah's vanishment had brought some sort of temporary peace to its walls. But now, with Rachel here, I knew it would not remain peaceful for long.

We had a late lunch of soup and canned spaghetti on toast, both more to Rachel's taste than mine. Rachel appeared thoughtful all through the meal. From time to time I would see her look up, as though she heard something, but when I asked her, she said no, there was nothing.

After lunch, we did a tour of the ground floor. The rooms were much larger than any Rachel had seen before, and she would go into each one admiringly, craning her neck to see the high ceilings. In the study, she stood very quiet for a while, then turned to me, pointing at the mantelpiece.

"There used to be funny lights there," she said. "Grandpa would set them on fire every night."

"Do you mean oil lamps?" I asked. There would not have been gas this far out in Catherine Trevorrow's time.

"I don't know. What are oil lamps like?"

"Well, did they have a tall glass piece on top, like a chimney?"

She frowned, then nodded.

"Yes. And shiny underneath. And there was a thing on the side you had to turn to make the light go up and down. I was never allowed to touch them."

Later, in the hall, she tugged my sleeve.

"What is it, Rachel?"

"Over there," she said. She was pointing at the wall opposite the staircase, just between the kitchen and the study.

"There used to be a little door there," she said.

"A door? But there's no room for it to go into."

She shook her head.

"It was a big cupboard. Things were kept in there. Brushes and things like that. I didn't like it. It was dark, and there were spiderwebs. Once, I got shut in by mistake, and cried and cried until I was let out."

Outside, it had started to grow dark. With the approach of night, the wind was rising. I could hear it in the trees. We went out in order to see the gardens before the light quite faded. Away from the house, Rachel reverted to an approximation of her former self. Here in the open air, it was as if a burden had been lifted from her small heart. I took her down to the cliff top, but she shrank back from it. The sound of the sea frightened her. This was the first time she had ever been to the coast. In this life.

Back inside, I let her watch television for a while. I had brought a portable set from London, knowing Rachel would be in need of distraction. It provided her with a world she could relate to. There were cartoons and songs and friendly faces. Nothing here could awaken memories of a past century. The television was an anchor chaining her to the present. I felt compelled to stay with her. I dared not let her out of my sight, not for a moment.

We went on watching television after the adult programs started. Rachel was initially intrigued, for the news and the soaps that followed it had until then been forbidden territory to her. But she grew quickly bored, and I suggested some games in the kitchen.

We played Ludo and Snakes and Ladders, and Rachel beat me every time, bursting into peals of laughter when she did so. But already she showed signs of growing tired. I was putting off bedtime. Now I was here, now it was night, now the wind outside had grown loud and sinister: the thought of climbing those too-familiar stairs and lying in that cold bedroom waiting for God knows what filled me with dread.

I made another meal, real pasta this time, with a passable Bolognese sauce. By the end, Rachel was growing genuinely tired. But I still hung back from going upstairs.

At nine o'clock she fell fast asleep in her chair. I could resist no longer. I switched off the lights, leaving on only those that lit the passage and the stairs. They would stay lit all night. Picking up Rachel, I held her across my shoulder and started up the stairs. God knows, I would not do that again. I was in a cold sweat by the time I reached the first landing. The noise of the storm beating in from the sea seemed to have brought the house to life. I thought that every bang and every rattle was a sign that it was beginning.

I had left the gas fire on in the room, and it was reasonably warm and dry. Rather than waken her, I let Rachel sleep in her clothes. I tucked her into bed, then slipped off my shirt and slipped into mine, leaving a low light lit on the bedside table. I kept my trousers on. Just in case. With the help of the lamp, I began to read.

Around midnight, I started to feel drowsy, though I was still reluctant to give way to sleep. I closed my book and sat upright, closing my eyes every so often, but without switching out the light. The meter had been well fed, there was no danger of the electricity being cut off. Unless the storm . . . I preferred not to think of that. But just in case, I had brought several flashlights with me.

Beside me, Rachel had started to murmur in her sleep. I looked across at her. Her arms were thrown out of the bedclothes, and her head was moving in small jerks from side to side. As I watched, the movements grew more violent. She was talking in her sleep, the words mumbled and incoherent. I decided to risk waking her. Pulling aside the bedclothes, I swung my legs out.

Suddenly Rachel screamed loudly and jerked herself upright. I thought she was about to go into convulsions. Racing across to her, I put my arms around her. She was wide-awake. Her breath was coming in short, rapid bursts.

"It's all right, love," I said. "It's all right, I'm here."

Her eyes were big with fear. What had she been dreaming of? She looked around the room frantically, then at me. I could smell the sudden fear.

"She's here," she said. "She's here in the house."

CHAPTER 25

IT WAS ONLY THEN that I realized the storm had passed. It must have died down unnoticed while I was half dozing. All the loud bumps and scrapes had vanished with it. The house was as silent as it had ever been, and as full of shadows. I sat there, holding Rachel in my arms and listening.

"Do you know where she is?" I whispered. I did not say the name. I think we both understood whom Rachel had meant.

Rachel shook her head. For the first time she was really frightened.

"But you know she is in the house?"

She nodded. I did not ask how she knew.

"Where is Catherine's mother?" I asked. I had determined to keep the identity of Rachel and Catherine separate if I could. I needed to know what I was dealing with. And I sensed that this was where the greatest danger lay, in a blurring of identities.

"Not here," Rachel said. Again, I did not demand to know the source of her knowledge. But I did not for a moment doubt that she was right.

That was when I heard a sound like creaking on the stairs. As though someone was outside, moving slowly. I felt myself go rigid with fright. All my senses were strained. Had the sound been above or below the floor we were on? I listened hard. Suddenly a door slammed somewhere. Then all the doors in the house started to close, one after the other. She was going from room to room. *Bang*. Silence. *Bang*. *Bang*.

The door of the bedroom started to open. Rachel and I were petrified. We did not know what was about to enter the room. The soft bedside light cast only a weak glow in the direction of the doorway. Slowly, the door swung open. A blast of cold air rushed into the room. I caught sight of something, but before I could see more closely, the door slammed shut again. Moments later another door down the corridor banged. She was still searching. But for what? Not for us. Now the banging moved to the top floor. We sat listening, shaking with cold. I held Rachel close and did my best to calm her. A last bang, then everything fell silent.

"Has she gone?" I asked.

Rachel shook her head.

A long silence followed. We did not move. I kept looking around the room, expecting to see something. But the shadows remained motionless.

All of a sudden the banging started again, but not slowly as before. Door after door banged in quick succession, ours among them. No sooner had the last door crashed shut than the sequence started again. *Bang. Bang. Bang. Bang. Bang.* And again. *Bang. Bang. Bang. Bang. Bang.* And again. It seemed as though it would go on all night.

But then, as suddenly as it had started, the banging stopped. The whole house seemed to be shaking from the violence of it. I could still hear the crashes in my head, like echoes ringing up and down the stairs. Rachel was clinging tightly to me. I could feel her tiny heart beating against my chest. My own heart was racing.

I bent down to Rachel.

"Has she gone this time?" I asked.

Again she shook her head. And again we waited.

The sound was not clear at first. More like a dull ache somewhere in the back of the mind, coming to consciousness only by degrees.

"Can you hear something?" I asked Rachel.

She nodded.

I strained my ears, desperate to make out what it was. Through the thin partition wall, I could make out what seemed to be the sound of someone moving restlessly on a bed. The creaking of the bedsprings was unmistakable. It was not the rhythmic sound of a couple making love. There would be a rustling noise, then the sound of springs, then silence for a few moments until it began again.

I do not know how long it continued. But there came a point when I knew I could not bear listening to it any longer. I had to do something.

Taking Rachel with me, I went to the door and opened it. The corridor was full of light. We stepped outside and crept to the door of the next room. I could feel my heart beating frantically. It took all my courage to put my hand on the handle and turn it.

The room was in darkness. But the sound of someone tossing and turning was clearer than ever. With a shaking hand, I switched on the light.

The bed was covered with a mass of tangled sheets, as though someone had been sleeping there and had just gotten up. Except that the sound had not stopped. It went on, though the bed was quite still, as if sight and sound existed in different places or different times.

And then, to my horror, I noticed that the bed was not quite still after all. As I watched I saw that something was slowly taking shape beneath the sheets. They had begun to move in a deliberate, revolting fashion, as though something unspeakable was writhing beneath them. I could not take my eyes off the bed. The shape continued to grow and to define itself, always writhing, always twisting. And with it the sound of a body tossing on springs. It was then that it started to lift what seemed to be a head, and I knew it was about to sit up in the bed. At the thought of it sitting there, staring at me, my nerve broke. I snatched Rachel up in my arms and ran headlong from the room.

At that instant all the lights in the house went out. In my nervousness on leaving the bedroom, I had forgotten to bring the flashlight with me. It was pitch-dark. And in the pitch darkness, I could hear the sound of soft feet—or something like feet—on the floor of the bedroom we had just been in. A door slammed on the floor above us.

I froze for a moment, not knowing which way to turn. If I went back into my own bedroom, it might take an eternity to find and switch on my flashlight. And I no longer knew what I might find there waiting for me. The footsteps were approaching. Perhaps it was just my imagination, but something about them sounded wet. Slippery. Not at all human. It was freezing cold.

I picked Rachel up again and ran for the stairs. This time I did not hesitate. I continued to run down, then along the hall to the front door. The next moment I had opened the door and dashed out into the night. The car keys were in my trouser pocket. That seemed the longest moment, fumbling with them while, at my back, I could hear footsteps on the stairs.

I pushed Rachel inside, then followed her and started the engine. I did not stop driving until we reached the road. We spent the night in a rest area with the engine running to keep us warm. I did not sleep.

CHAPTER 26

WE RETURNED to the house about an hour after dawn. Neither of us wanted to be there, but I knew that if we left, matters would never be brought to a head. Rachel was very tired, but she seemed less affected by the events of the previous night than I.

"I'm hungry," she said. "Can we have breakfast?"

"Of course. Two breakfasts coming up." I was starving, too.

In the clear light of day, the terrors of the night seemed nebulous. What had there been, after all? Just some sounds, what may have been a figure in a doorway, crumpled sheets moving on a bed. Surely nothing threatening or dangerous in any of that. And yet I was still nervous, and every so often caught myself looking over my shoulder.

The smell of bacon and eggs filled the kitchen. There was something so frankly normal about the smell and the appearance of the food on our plates that I felt the shadows lifting. After all, I reasoned, was this not why I had returned to Petherick House in the first place, to confront whatever unease lay at the heart of these hauntings and, if possible, put it to rest? I decided that we would spend that day searching for the remains of Catherine Trevorrow. They were here somewhere, of that I was certain. It was only a matter of finding them. I had an idea that Rachel might be drawn to them somehow, that that was what Susannah wanted.

To add to the sense of normality, I switched on the radio I had brought with me. Light music had its uses, I thought. Rachel seemed to know half the singers and half the songs. The deejay's voice could not have been more out of place or more welcome. I opened the backdoor. Rachel went into the garden to play; I gave her strict instructions not to stray from my sight.

There was a news broadcast at nine o'clock. The usual things: loud exchanges on the floor of the House of Commons, some trouble concerning the Falkland Islands, a scandal involving an MP. Toward the end, there was a short piece of more immediate interest.

"A search is still continuing for novelist Peter Clare and a four-year-old girl he is thought to have abducted, Rachel Wigram. Mr. Clare, the author of seven novels and two collections of short stories, is understood to have taken Rachel from the Radcliffe Infirmary in Oxford, where the child's parents had been taken following a car crash on Monday. The couple, Tim and Susan Wigram of Brondesbury in London, both died later in hospital. In the meantime, Mr. Clare, who is said to have been a friend of the family, had made arrangements to return with the child to London, where he has a flat.

"Rachel's grandparents, who had been on holiday in

Spain, returned to England yesterday. On trying to make contact with their granddaughter, they found that both she and Mr. Clare had vanished.

"There are now fears that Rachel has been abducted. The Metropolitan Police revealed last night that Clare, aged forty-six, was convicted of manslaughter in 1970 following the violent death of his daughter, Catherine. He spent five years in prison. In an interview yesterday, Clare's sister-in-law, Lorna Trevor, suggested that he may be suffering from severe depression following the death of his wife, Sarah, who was drowned in an accident in Cornwall earlier this year.

"Clare is five foot ten with receding gray hair, slimly built, and clean-shaven. Rachel Wigram is four years old and has short blond hair and brown eyes. Anyone seeing them is requested to contact the nearest police station."

I looked up. Rachel was still in the garden playing unself-consciously with a ball. I made a bowl of cornflakes for her and sprinkled them with white sugar. We would need fresh milk later in the day. It was a nuisance, Tim's parents turning up like that. I had been banking on a couple of weeks at least. It need not make a real difference, of course. I should just have to be circumspect, that was all. Leaving Rachel alone in the house was unthinkable, naturally. If we went shopping, we would just have to go together and take the risk of being spotted. Or perhaps I could leave her in the car briefly while I raced around a supermarket, stocking up on imperishables. Dried milk, cans, pasta, and dried cereal. I had brought plenty of cash with me. There would be no need for visits to banks. But perhaps none of that would be necessary anyway.

It might all be over in a day or two, one way or another.

There was a Safeway just outside Penzance. I left Rachel in the car while I made enough purchases for a fortnight, reasoning that I could always take them back to London with me when this was all over. For good measure, I put about a dozen flashlights and a heap of batteries into my trolley. As far as I could tell, no one paid any particular notice to me as I walked around the shop. Why should they have? They would have been on the lookout for a man with a little girl. That's the way ordinary people's minds work. But who in Penzance would think for a moment that I would turn up on their doorstep?

There was a newspaper stand at the supermarket entrance. I tossed a few papers into my trolley, intending to read them afterward at my leisure. Only *The Sun* had me on the front page. A rare honor for a serious novelist. It was my most recent publicity photograph: not a very good likeness, I thought. I wondered who had given it to them.

I had bought treats for Rachel. How easy it is to please some children. The whiskey I justified to myself not as a treat, but as pure necessity. How could I stay in that awful place without it?

Rachel wanted to see the sea. We drove along, chanting the words in a silly singsong: "We're off to see the sea, we're off to see the sea." Out of season, the beaches at St. Ives were wet and deserted. I was able to take Rachel along with me, with little fear of discovery. She ran on the sand, picking up seaweed and throwing it into the wind. Out at sea, high waves crested and fell, crested and fell. And a white boat passed near the horizon and vanished into a gray fret.

Inland, I could see the slope of the little cemetery in which Susannah Trevorrow had been buried. Buried, but not laid to rest. It was not far from there to Zawn Quoits. A short walk would have taken Rachel and me there, but there was no pathway along the sea's edge.

The morning passed easily. By lunchtime, Rachel was starving again. I would have preferred to eat in a hotel or restaurant, anything rather than go back to Petherick House so soon, but that, of course, was out of the question. We drove back, growing silent as we came within sight of the place. In a few hours it would start to grow dark. Another night would begin.

After lunch, there was children's television. The electricity was working perfectly again, as though nothing had happened the night before. I checked the fuse box, but all seemed in order. And tonight I would not let go of my flashlight for anything.

While Rachel laughed at the antics of Duckula I sat in the corner reading. My life had been laid out in the tabloids for the whole country to read. Some of it was flattering, much of it quite the opposite. Not even *The Guardian* or *The Independent* had a high opinion of my books. The literary Mafia had their claws out as usual.

Clare's first novel, *Day of Wrath*, [wrote *The Guardian*] was written in prison and published shortly after his release in 1975. It was an attempt to exorcise the inner demons that had led to the brutal killing of his child under the influence of drink. The book made a powerful impact on publication, and Clare became a minor celebrity for a short time. Like John McVicar, he was lionized as an ex-convict turned literary wunderkind. His second book, *The House of Dark Visions*, did not fulfill the promise of the first, however. In the end, Clare's middle-class origins betrayed him. To many readers, he seemed more a self-indulgent brat who had engineered his own misfortunes and gone on to make literary capital from them, than a hardened criminal from the streets redeemed by education and the imaginative life. His later novels plowed much the same furrow as the first. Dead children, dead wives, guilt, remorse, the torment of the damned condemned to repeat their crimes.

I had a pretty good idea who'd written that little put-down. He'd been at one of my launches and stuffed himself with canapés without even bothering to pass the time of day with me or my publicity people.

I put down the last paper, clenching and unclenching my fists. A good thing I'd bought the whiskey—I needed a stiff drink to banish the taste of all that crap from my mouth. Rachel was still watching cartoons. I looked out the window. The mist that we had watched at sea earlier was now moving steadily inland. Petherick House would soon be cut off by more than the dark.

About four o'clock, we retired to the kitchen. I had put on all the lights by then and restocked the meter with coins. In each of the ground-floor rooms, I had placed a flashlight within easy reach, and I carried two around with me. Rachel had one of her own.

We laid the table for tea. I had bought *tarte tatin*, a French apple and caramel pie, that morning. We had it with cream. It was the first time Rachel had ever tasted it: she thought it was the most delicious thing she had ever eaten. There was milk for her and Gunpowder Green tea for me. The house was utterly quiet. Outside, it was pitch-dark.

"When is Christmas coming?" Rachel asked.

"Soon," I said, "very soon. You'll have to write a list for Father Christmas."

"Will we be here for Christmas?"

I shook my head.

"I don't think so," I answered.

"I want to go home for Christmas, otherwise Santa won't know where to find me. And Mummy and Daddy, too."

"We'll be home, I promise."

I looked around almost guiltily. What right had I to make promises in this place?

Suddenly I looked up. I could hear something. Had it begun? But as I listened the sound quickly resolved itself into something quite mundane, though nonetheless unsettling. It was the sound of a car coming down the drive.

We waited. The car drew to a halt outside the house. A door banged shut. Moments later someone knocked at the front door. I could not believe it. Had I been spotted after all? Had someone from Tredannack noticed that someone was living at Petherick House, and put two and two together?

I told Rachel to stay in the kitchen.

"Stay quiet," I told her.

"Who is it?"

"I don't know," I answered. But I was fairly sure it was the police. There was a louder knock at the door.

I crept into the study, from which I was able to get a clear view of the front without being seen. It was unpleasant, moving through that dark room, unable to light a flashlight. I looked through the window.

A car with a light on its roof was sitting outside with its engine running. My heart sank until I realized that it was not a police car but a taxi. I felt tremendous relief, followed by renewed anxiety. Who else knew there was someone here? The caller knocked heavily for about ten seconds.

There was no help for it. I went to the door and opened it.

In the darkness and mist, I did not recognize her for a moment. Then she stepped forward into the light from the hall. It was Susannah—Susannah Adderstone.

CHAPTER 27

She paid the taxi. As he drove off into the mist she turned and came back to the door, where I was still standing. Not a word had passed between us.

"I thought I'd find you here," she said.

"You know, then?"

She nodded gravely.

"I heard about it on the news yesterday. Father and I talked about you all last night. He was against my coming down, but I insisted. He says it's out of his hands now. I made him tell me all he knew. About what really happened here."

"And you still wanted to come, knowing that?"

She hesitated.

"Yes. You don't mind, do you?"

"Mind? It's not for me to mind. This is your house. Your father's, anyway."

I noticed that she had brought a small case.

"Let me take that for you. We can't stand here talking; it's freezing."

She stepped into the hallway, into the light. For the second time I was shocked by how beautiful she was. As she came in she glanced around at everything, as though reassuring herself that it was all real. I closed the door and helped her off with her coat.

"Let's go to the kitchen," I said. "I've just been having tea there with Rachel."

"How is the little girl?" asked Susannah.

"How did you expect her to be? Beaten up, maybe? Dead?"

"No, of course not, I . . ." She reddened.

"That's quite all right. Whatever the papers say, I'm not a murderer."

"I never thought you were." She paused. "Does Rachel . . . ? Have you told her about her parents yet?"

I shook my head.

"No, not yet," I replied. "There's all this to go through first."

"That's why I came, Peter. To tell you it's not too late to pull out of . . . whatever it is you think you're doing here. Rachel's safe. I can tell the police I sent you the keys to this place, that you told me you wanted to bring her down here for a break after the accident. They've no reason not to believe you."

Such blinding stupidity. As if I had come all the way here to leave this thing unfinished.

"It isn't possible," I said. "Something has started here; I have to finish it. Rachel knows what's happening; in some ways she knows more than anyone. Her memory is coming back. The house is acting on her, reawakening Catherine in her."

Susannah looked frightened.

"Perhaps you should leave," I said. "It's not too late. I can drive you back to Penzance."

She shook her head.

"I'm part of this thing, too," she said. With a smile, she took a step toward the kitchen. "Come on, it's time I met Rachel."

I followed her. The moment I stepped through the door, I knew something was wrong. Susannah looked at me, puzzled. The smile had faded. The table was still laid for tea. The pot of tea and the half-drunk glass of milk were still there. But Rachel had vanished.

Susannah was the first to notice that the backdoor was lying ajar. I thrust a flashlight into her hand and led the way into the darkness outside. It was bitterly cold; any warmth there had been in the air had been sucked from it by the mist. Even with the flashlight, I could see only a few feet in any direction.

"Rachel!" I shouted. "Where are you? Can you hear me?"

There was no answer. I looked around. The lights of the house had already disappeared into the mist somewhere behind us. Or was it to the side? I was already growing disoriented.

"Peter, she may not be out here at all." Susannah was still close to me.

"The door was open," I said. "And we would have seen her if she'd come down the passage from the kitchen. You would have seen her—you were facing that way. She has to be out here."

"But surely she wouldn't have gone far. Not in this."

"She's four years old, Susannah. There's no knowing what she may do. Once she got into the mist, she would have lost her way in seconds. She could be anywhere."

As I said the words I heard a sound that made my heart shrivel. Waves slapping a cliff face, waves coming in fast. If Rachel were to walk that way, she could miss the cliff edge in the mist and crash to her death. I resumed shouting with all my strength.

"Rachel! Are you out there? Answer me!"

But the only sound that came back to me was the crashing of waves.

"Stay beside me," I said. "We can't afford to get separated from each other."

I saw Susannah halt.

"Peter." Her voice was strained, awkward. "I want you to tell me the truth. Has something already happened to Rachel? Has there already been an accident? Because, if there has, this is just a charade, and I don't want anything more to do with it."

I could not see her. When I spoke, I did so in the direction of the light she was holding.

"You saw the milk on the table. And you know it hadn't been put there for your benefit."

"I'm not saying she was never here. Just that . . . something may have happened, something you didn't intend. Like before . . ."

If she had not been hidden, I might have struck her. But it was only a voice, I told myself, only a voice. I turned and walked on into the mist. Susannah could look after herself.

As I started walking I heard a sound. A child's voice. It was Rachel, calling from quite near at hand.

"Rachel? Stay where you are! Do you hear me? Don't move. Just keep calling. Do you understand?"

"Yes." She sounded very frightened.

"Keep calling, and I'll come and get you. I'm not far away."

Rachel was an intelligent child. She did exactly as I told her. It took about ten minutes to grope my way to her through the mist. Time and again I thought I had her, only to find that something had distorted her voice or given me a false sense of the direction from which it was coming. And then, suddenly, there she was, standing shivering on the grass in front of me.

I picked her up in my arms and held her close for a long time. Just as I set her down I heard a voice behind me.

"I'm sorry, Peter. It was wrong of me not to believe you."

Susannah must have followed the light of my flashlight. Her own was switched off. Now she turned it back on again.

I introduced her to Rachel.

"This is Susannah," I said. "That's who came to the door earlier. She's come to stay for a few days. Her daddy owns Petherick House."

Rachel seemed unimpressed.

"I'm cold," she said.

"We're all cold, love. It's freezing out here. Let's get back to the house."

But that was easier to say than to do. Petherick House had been swallowed up entirely by the mist, and I had no idea which direction it lay in. The sound of waves was the only guide we had to the location of anything. We could try walking away from it, but that might as easily send us right on past the house as into it. One thing was certain: we could not spend the night outside. None of us was dressed for it. There was a real danger that we would all die from exposure.

I do not know how long we stumbled about there. All I can remember is the mist writhing through the dark while all the time I grew colder and weaker. I could feel Rachel shivering against me as I held her in my arms, trying to press some warmth into her. The batteries of our flashlights were rapidly losing their first strength. Not that they helped a great deal anyway. What little they showed of the terrain across which we were walking was of absolutely no use in establishing our position.

Susannah was the first to catch sight of the light.

"Look!"

I saw her pointing up at what we knew could only be a light from the house. The next moment it was wiped from sight by a great hand of mist. And then the mist moved on, and we could see the light as clearly as before. With a cry of triumph, I started for it. Susannah followed.

As we neared the house—which had not, after all, been very far away—other lights became visible. At the last moment a bank of mist rolled away, uncovering the entire rear of the building. It was only then that I realized that the light we had been following had not been, as I had thought, a downstairs light, but one in an upstairs room. In a room in the top floor, to be precise. Susannah Trevorrow's bedroom, to be more precise again.

As our feet touched the gravel path that circled the house, the light flickered and went out.

It took us a long time to get warm again. While Susannah watched Rachel in the kitchen I ventured upstairs alone to fetch some quilts. It was silent up there. Silent and dark.

As I was taking the quilt from my bed, I glanced across the room. Rachel's bed had been made up first thing that morning. But something seemed odd about it. I went across and looked down.

On the pillow lay a doll. A doll in a sailor suit, identical to the one I had burned in London. It almost seemed to glare at me as I picked it up and shoved it under my own bed.

Downstairs again, I made hot soup and poured it

into mugs for us to hold. Bit by bit, we thawed out. Seeing one of the whiskey bottles, Susannah suggested hot toddies. I found some sugar and powdered cinnamon I had bought to put on hot chocolate for Rachel. The toddies—large ones for Susannah and myself, a much smaller one for Rachel—warmed us from top to bottom.

As we grew more relaxed I took Rachel on my knee. I saw Susannah watching us. Had our discovery of Rachel, safe and sound after all, restored her trust in me? Or was she still like all the others, unbelieving and afraid?

"Darling," I said to Rachel, "you must never ever do that again. If you go outside in the dark, you can have an accident. A bad accident. I've already shown you the big cliff at the bottom of the garden, haven't I? You wouldn't want to fall over there, would you?"

She shook her head. She seemed troubled about something.

"What is it, Rachel? You can tell me, I'm not angry."

She hesitated, then began to speak.

"I'm sorry I went out," she said. "But she said it would be all right."

I felt the skin on the back of my neck go cold.

"She? Do you mean your aunt Agnes?"

She shook her head.

"No," she said. "The little girl. The little girl who came to the door when you were out. She wanted to play. She said you wouldn't mind."

CHAPTER 28

WE HAD AN early supper. After eating, we headed for the main room, what our Mrs. Rudd from Truro would have called "the parlor." I proposed to Susannah that she join me in drinking more of the whiskey, not in a toddy this time, but in glasses, neat.

"I've had enough already, thanks. Spirits go to my head."

"Do you mind if I have one?"

"Of course not; go ahead."

Rachel amused herself with a bunch of coloring books and felt-tipped pens I had bought for her in Safeway. Every so often, she would bring a page across for us to admire.

"She's a lovely child," said Susannah. "It's a pity about . . ."

I stopped her with a frown.

"We can talk about that later," I said. "I think perhaps it's your turn to tell me a little about yourself."

She had studied as an interior designer and worked for a couple of years in London before going back to Yorkshire to look after her father.

"Like your namesake," I said.

"My great-aunt? Yes, I suppose so. But I never had a sister. I was an only child. It makes Father all the more my responsibility."

"Aren't there other relatives?"

There was a moment's hesitation before she answered. She shook her head, spilling her hair across one shoulder.

"No one close. It's up to me, really."

"Don't you have anyone else? I mean, a boyfriend or . . . someone in London."

I realized that I knew absolutely nothing about her. She might have been married, divorced, widowed, the mother of three children . . . anything.

She laughed.

"No. There hasn't been a man in my life for some time."

"I can't believe that. Why, you're . . ." I hesitated, knowing it was taking a risk. "You're really very lovely."

She blushed.

"Now you're embarrassing me," she said. But I could see that she had not been displeased.

"No," I said, encouraged. "I do mean it. It's hard to believe you don't have men fighting over you."

She said nothing to that. Rachel came over with another completed drawing. She had taken a perfectly innocent cow standing in a field and transformed it into a purple space monster surrounded by what must have been its victims.

"It's beautiful," I said. "It looks just like me."

She giggled and went off to desecrate another page of the book.

"Tell me about your daughter," Susannah said. "The one who died."

What other one had there ever been? It was a direct question, but she must have known how hard it would be for me to answer. I swallowed the whiskey that was left in my glass and poured myself another.

"You've read the book," I said. "You know it all already."

"No, that's just what everybody knows. I want to hear it from you. Face-to-face."

I looked at her. What did she really want with me?

"She was almost four years old, Rachel's age. A very beautiful child. I still have dreams of her. In some ways, Rachel reminds me of her. They look a little alike."

"How did she die?"

"I'd had too much to drink. You'll have read that, of course. I drank because I was unhappy, and I was unhappy because life wasn't what life should have been. Maybe you can't understand that, I don't know. I'd given up my school job to try my hand as a writer, but it hadn't worked out. There were no school places to go back to, so I took a job as a language teacher. English for foreign students. It was all I could find. Maybe it was all I was qualified to do. By the end of the first year, I'd had enough, but there was nothing else, and I began to think there never would be. Sarah wasn't working then, so I had to keep at it. Day after day, the same idiotic examples of the same idiotic grammatical rules. 'Where a verb is used with more than one auxiliary, make sure that the main verb is repeated.' '"Require" should not be used as an intransitive verb in the sense of "need."' I started drinking just to keep going."

I paused and, as if on cue, took another mouthful from my glass.

"One night I had a pile of essays to mark for a class early the next morning. I was marking them in the kitchen with Catherine. They were full of the usual stupid mistakes. As usual, I was drinking. I suppose I was drunk, I can't remember. I'm not certain what happened next. There was a pot of . . . red paint. . . . Catherine had little pots of them. She . . . spilled it over the essays. I . . . lost my temper. Hit her. I didn't mean to, not like that. Not so hard. The blow sent her backward into a glass door. We'd always told her to be careful of that door. I remember thinking at first that she'd spilled more paint, that I would have to hit her again. And then I realized what I'd done."

I looked across at her. She was so achingly beautiful, and what I was telling her was so ugly.

"I'd like to stop talking about this. It brings back memories. I . . ."

"Don't get upset. I'm sorry. I shouldn't have asked."

We fell silent. A shadow had come between us. I saw Susannah glancing from me to Rachel and back again. Rachel looked up. She had grown tired of drawing. "Can we watch a video?" she asked.

"We don't have a machine here," I said. "And in any case, you're getting tired, young lady. I think it's time for bed."

Having Susannah there made the thought of returning up those stairs a little less daunting. I turned to her.

"I think we should all go up. Rachel can't stay here on her own. You can have the bed in the room we were in last night. It's quite comfortable." I glanced at Rachel. "Rachel, you won't mind if Susannah spends the night with you, will you?"

She shook her head, yawning, not really interested.

"What about you?" Susannah asked.

"I'll be all right. There's a bed in the room next

door." I was not thinking of the room in which I had seen that thing the previous night, but one on the other side, where a lot of old furniture was kept.

"If you're sure."

"I can always shout if anything happens. It's not myself I'm worried about. It's Rachel. She's at the center of all this."

Susannah carried Rachel upstairs and undressed her for bed while I busied myself with the quilts. Mr. Belkins had not put in a reappearance. I glanced under the larger bed: the doll was no longer there. Someone was playing games.

"There are flashlights and batteries here," I said, showing my treasures to Susannah. "We had a failure last night, so there's a chance you'll need them."

"I don't mind if you stay in here," she said. "It's not as if . . ."

I smiled and thanked her.

"I'd sooner not. I might be unable to stop-myself making a pass at you. And then where would we be?"

She laughed, rather awkwardly I thought. As if she was not altogether accustomed to the idea of men making passes at her.

I said good night to both of them and went off to my room, carrying a box of flashlights in my arms, like a small boy off to his first scout camp, frightened of the dark.

The first thing I did after lighting the gas fire was to pour myself another glass of whiskey. My box had contained more than flashlights and batteries. Well, why not? It was going to be a long night, and I was badly in need of some Dutch courage.

Apart from the bed, the room contained a heavy oak wardrobe, a small table with a bowl and pitcher, both empty and covered in dust, a desk, and a bedside table.

Sitting near the fire with my whiskey in one hand, I kept my eye on the door. I expected that awful banging to start at any moment, and to see the door thrown open and slammed shut again a dozen times or more. I was bracing myself for it. But the house remained obstinately still. As though it, too, was waiting.

From time to time my eyes strayed to the wardrobe. It had a faintly malevolent air, and I could not keep myself from imagining that something unpleasant lurked inside it. It was not long before the thought of the wardrobe and what it might contain started to prey on my mind almost more heavily than any horror occasioned by the door.

In the end, I could stand it no longer. Downing two fingers of whiskey to stiffen my resolve, I got to my feet and yanked open the wardrobe door.

It was empty, save for a couple of old wooden hangers swinging from a central rail. As I made to close the door again I noticed that, after all, there was something there. Almost out of sight, a cardboard box had been pushed back along a shelf in the upper right corner.

I lifted it down and carried it across to the desk. It seemed to be an old hatbox, and for all I knew, it contained nothing but an old hat. It was not very heavy. I lifted off the lid.

Inside were dozens of photographs, most of them pasted to stiff backing cards, many of them the product of a studio in St. Ives in the last decades of the nineteenth century. Had they been left here by the late Agnes Trevorrow? It seemed the most likely explanation for their presence here.

I started to go through them. Right away I noticed that someone had written on their backs in a fine copperplate hand, giving the names of those portrayed, with the date of the sittings in most cases. They were in no particular order.

Here was a stiff studio portrait of Jeremiah Trevorrow, dressed in his best clothes and looking decidedly ill at ease: *My father, Jeremiah, aged 45. Taken in 1875 by Mr. Barilari at St. Ives.* My guess was right, then: these had belonged to Agnes. Beneath the photograph of her father lay one of an attractive young woman in a high-necked dress. The inscription on the back read: *The whore Susannah's mother, Esther, may she rot. Taken in her last year, 1880.*

Many of the inscriptions were like that, full of unspent rancor. The sitters seemed to stare at me out of the past, trapped little creatures making mute appeals for help. I lifted them from the box one by one. They were musty and unpleasant to the touch.

Suddenly there was a piercing shriek. A child started to cry somewhere outside my room. I got up, scattering the photographs, and made for the door.

CHAPTER 29

Susannah was already at the door of the main bedroom. She was wearing a white nightgown. I rushed up to her.

"What's going on?" I asked. "Is Rachel all right?"

"She's fine. She's still sleeping. The noise hasn't woken her, thank God."

"But I thought . . ."

She did not answer. As we both listened it became clear that the crying was coming not from the bedroom as I had at first thought, but from somewhere higher up—somewhere on the next floor. And I realized where I had heard it before: on a tape in the police station in St. Ives.

Suddenly the crying stopped. There was a sound of feet pattering on the stairs, a child's feet. A woman's voice called out: "Catherine. Catherine." But we could see no one. The house began to fill with silence again.

Shaken, I returned to the bedroom with Susannah.

Rachel was still asleep, but tossing from side to side now, as though in considerable distress.

"Shouldn't we waken her?" Susannah asked.

But even as she spoke Rachel grew calm and began to settle down again. Within moments her breathing became more regular, her movements less violent. Soon she was quiet again—the perfect image of a sleeping child. Susannah bent down and stroked her forehead. Rachel did not stir.

"I have something to show you," I said.

She looked up at me curiously.

"It's next door," I said. "You stay here and keep an eye on Rachel. Call me if she seems distressed. But I won't be long anyway."

The photographs were lying on the floor where they had fallen. I bent down and started picking them up in small bundles, putting them back into the box at random. There did not seem to have been order to them in the first place.

As I did so one photograph drew my attention. It was a studio portrait of a young couple. The man was dressed in the garb of a late Victorian ecclesiastic. He seemed rather smug and self-righteous to me. His posture was redolent of rectitude and the virtues of the cloth. But it was less the man than the woman who had drawn me.

She had on a long plain dress and a small bonnet without lace. Her eyes stared straight into mine, almost with a look of recognition. There was a shadow across one cheek, the indistinct pattern of a port-wine mark, marring her face. But the face—apart from the stain—was quite lovely. Lovely and familiar. It was Susannah Adderstone's face: her eyes, her nose, her mouth—the face of the woman I had been speaking to only moments earlier.

I felt my hands tremble as I turned the photograph

over. *Rev. Sowerby and myself on the day of our engagement, 10 June 1883.*

He must have known. Her father. My meek-mannered Mr. Adderstone must have seen more than one photograph of his aunt as a young woman. I wondered when it had first struck him. When Susannah was twelve? Fourteen? Sixteen? When had the moment of recognition come? Or had he guessed from the start? Was that why he had called her Susannah, in a vain attempt to ward off what must have seemed to him like a curse? *My aunt, Mr. Clare, was the most evil human being I have ever known.* I could hear his voice, saying the words over and over again. And Rachel's voice the night before: *She's here. She's here in the house.*

My whiskey glass was still on the desk. I lifted it and gulped down a mouthful. I don't think I have ever needed a drink so badly in my life. I tilted the bottle and refilled the glass. With a hand that still trembled, I turned the photograph over again. How she had fooled me all the time. The plain, the deformed Agnes Trevorrow: who would have seen her face in the beautiful features of Susannah Adderstone?

A long time passed, I don't know how long. I sat there, staring at the photograph and sipping whiskey. I had opened the door. I had let her in: Susannah . . . Agnes. My mind was reeling, I was growing more and more confused.

I heard a noise outside the door. Footsteps. I turned. Fear was making me sober again. I remembered that Rachel was next door, alone with Susannah.

Cursing my stupidity for letting so much time pass, I flung the door open and dashed into the corridor. It was empty. I ran to the next room. The door was wide open. I ran in, but there was no one there. Susannah and Rachel had both gone.

I hurried back down the passage to the head of

the stairs. Something made me look up, just in time to catch sight of them as they reached the next landing and disappeared around the corner. I lunged for the stairs, but as I did so the lights blacked out and I fell headlong across the bottom steps, winding myself.

By the time I recovered and switched on the flashlight which I carried on a cord around my neck, Susannah and Rachel were well out of sight. Frantically, I staggered up the stairs. As I did so the doors started to crash shut. *Bang, bang, bang, bang.* They began at the bottom and followed me up the stairs. *Bang, bang, bang, bang, bang.* She was here, I could feel her and hear her moving through the dark house. *Bang, bang, bang, bang, bang.*

I reached the top landing. Flashing the light down the passage, I could see no one. They must have gone into one of the rooms. I did not have to guess which one. In a state of growing panic, I ran down to the last room and grabbed the door handle, pushing inward as I did so.

The door did not move. It was as solid as a rock. I tried again, much harder this time, twisting and turning the handle, but it remained firmly locked against me. Stepping back, I played the light across the surface of the door. At the top and bottom, it had been bolted and padlocked shut.

Someone laughed softly, just to my left. I swung around, throwing the beam of the flashlight in that direction. She was there, standing triumphantly a few feet away, a sneering smile on her wrinkled face. *My aunt, Mr. Clare, was the most evil human being I have ever known.*

Something told me she would not try to stop me. She was done with me, or so she thought. With a cry, I ran at her. I felt nothing as I passed through, hurtling for the head of the stairs. I could hear nothing but the sound of my own feet pounding as I dashed down, taking the stairs two and three at a time. I fell twice, all but breaking my neck. With so much whiskey in my veins, it is a wonder that I did not.

There was a cupboard in the kitchen that held some tools. I found what I had come for: the ax that had been set aside for chopping firewood. I would not let her defeat me, not so easily.

Panting, I hared back up the dark stairs with all the speed I could muster. I didn't know how much she could see or hear, or whether she was even interested. All I did know was that I had to get to Rachel before something irreparable happened—if it had not done so already. This had not been how I had planned things. Everything was sliding out of control.

The house shook. I don't know how else to describe it. It was as though an earthquake had tossed it around for half a second. The force of the convulsion threw me full against the stairs, winding me. No sooner had I gotten to my feet than there was a second shudder. This time I was ready for it. A third and a fourth blow followed as I went on climbing, then the house suddenly grew still again.

I reached the door. It was locked as before. Taking a deep breath, I crashed the ax into the wood, just above the bottom bolt. The sound rang through the house. I swung the ax and struck hard again. The wood cracked and splintered, groaning under the shock of the blows I dealt it, but it would not give way. The locks held to the very last.

Abruptly, a final blow sent the door swinging crazily on its hinges. I stood, ax in hand, on the threshold of a half-dark room.

*   *   *

I stepped inside. The room had changed since I had last set foot in it. An oil lamp stood on the mantelpiece among framed photographs and little ornaments. On the papered walls hung little prints and a text, *Thou, Lord, Seest Me.* A large bed stood against one wall. On it lay Rachel in her pajamas. Beside her on a low chair sat Susannah, staring straight ahead, but seeing nothing. Or perhaps seeing things I could not see.

I knew I had to get Rachel out of there. I started forward, but as I did so I realized that I had come too late.

CHAPTER 30

SHE WAS IN the room with us. I felt her before I saw her. Her presence in that dark room was like thick, raw fear. It lay in my throat like poison, choking me. My mind felt horribly confused. It was a magic room, or so it seemed then. In it nothing else and nowhere else mattered. The whole world had gone.

When I looked at Rachel again, she seemed to have shifted, to have changed, and I knew that the child on the bed was no longer Rachel but my own daughter, Catherine, Catherine whom I had killed all those years ago. She looked at me with fear in her eyes. I could feel the ax in my hand, heavy and light at the same time. I took a step toward the bed.

Catherine screamed, and suddenly it was no longer my daughter but another child, a little girl crouching naked and defenseless with her back to the wall. And when I looked again, it was Rachel, and I was lifting the ax in my hand.

Out of nowhere a figure appeared in front of me. I recognized her. It was Sarah, dressed in the same clothes she had been wearing on the night of her vanishment. She held her hands out toward me, and suddenly it was no longer Sarah but Susannah Trevorrow, pleading with me not to kill her child. I could feel the ax in my hand like a fever, burning me.

I shook my head. But at that moment there was a crashing sound. On the bed, Rachel was having convulsions. Her whole body was being flung up and down with the most terrible violence. The bed was crashing, harder, harder, harder. The room had started to fill with flying objects: pictures and ornaments and fragments of broken wood from the door. Cracks appeared in the walls and ceiling. Suddenly there was a tremendous explosion. All the glass in all the windows of the house had shattered simultaneously. The house itself started to shake again, not momentarily this time, but in steady, rhythmic shudders.

Susannah Trevorrow was beside me, mouthing her entreaties. Tears were streaming down her face. Then it was Sarah's face, looking up at me as she had looked at me that night she found our daughter dead. Her mouth opened and closed, but I could hear nothing, not a sound.

The cold air streaming into the room seemed to clear my brain. I knew I had to do something to stop what was happening, to stop the cycle from repeating. I looked around desperately. Agnes Trevorrow was standing near the door, as though orchestrating everything. Her eyes were filled with a look of utter malice, malice so implacable I thought she would destroy the world to wreak the evil she so much wanted.

As I tore my eyes away I caught sight of something on the wall opposite the fireplace. A large patch of damp. The sight of it stirred a memory in me. I remembered the paintings Sarah had left behind, the hand in them, pressed against the wallpaper.

Without pausing, I stepped to the wall and lifted the ax. There was a howl of anger behind me. But I did not falter. I brought the ax down hard in the center of the damp patch. Plaster cracked and fell away. I raised the ax and brought it down again. She was there, her mouth working, her eyes wide with fear and anger, but I ignored her, smashing the ax into the wall for a third time. Something came tumbling out of the hole I had made. I looked down. It was a doll. A china doll dressed in a sailor suit. It was covered in dust and cobwebs, but it was still recognizable as the doll Rachel called Mr. Belkins.

I struck the wall harder. With every blow, more plaster came away. And then, all at once, a section gave completely and something else came falling from the cavity behind. I shuddered as I looked down. It was a bundle of bones, and a tiny skull with long hair matted to it.

I scarcely know what happened next. There was a terrible cry. Agnes Trevorrow began to fade before my eyes. I dropped the ax. I watched her clutch the air. All around her, mist was weaving patterns, working its way into the room through the smashed window. Moments later she was gone.

When I looked down, Rachel was lying on the floor, perfectly still. Near her, Susannah Trevorrow stood watching me. She was smiling. I have never seen anyone so lovely or so radiant. Seconds after, she had disappeared and in her place I saw Sarah standing surrounded by mist. She stepped across to me and, just for an instant, I could feel her lips against mine. Then she, too, was gone.

I closed my eyes and sank down onto the floor. I must have remained like that for half a minute or more. When I opened my eyes again, the room had filled more than ever with mist. We would have to leave, get downstairs and into the car. I looked across to where Susannah was sitting, facing me.

Her eyes were fixed on mine. I smiled, but she did not return my smile.

"It's over," I said. "She's gone."

At that moment Rachel opened her eyes and pulled herself upright. I smiled across at her. She too did not smile back.

"It's all right now, love. We're going to be leaving soon. Back to London."

She looked at me, and I could see that she was still frightened. And then my heart stood still, for I could tell that she was frightened of something in the room.

"She's still here," Rachel said. "She hasn't gone."

I have never felt so cold. I looked around at the broken door, but Agnes was not there. And then I caught Susannah's eyes again, and I understood. The look of malice, of absolute, all-consuming hatred was as strong in them as it had ever been. And it was then that I noticed that Susannah was holding something very bright and very sharp. I recognized it as a carving knife, one of a set that had been kept in the kitchen drawer.

Quick as a cat, she leapt to her feet and turned toward Rachel.

I did not think. I just moved. I picked up the ax, staggering to my feet as I did so, and in a single motion swept the blade in an arc whose center was Susannah's neck. It was not a perfect cut, but it did not have to be perfect.

CHAPTER 31

I HAD TWO MORE things to do that night. The first was to go downstairs and break open the old cupboard that Agnes had boarded up, the one between the kitchen and the study. What I found there I wrapped in sheets the next morning, after the mist had cleared. I took the bundles down to the cliff and threw them into the sea. It was better no one knew. Tredannack and its inhabitants would not rest any easier for being told.

During the night, I took the bones of Catherine Trevorrow and put them in a small wooden box. Rachel came with me. We drove to St. Ives and found Susannah's grave again. This time I had brought my own spade. I uncovered the coffin for the second time and, opening it, lifted the bones from the box and laid them among Susannah's. They are there now, and I pray they rest undisturbed until the sea eats the shore away at last.

Rachel and I drove back to London the following

morning. I can still remember the look of astonishment on the policeman's face when I came into the station to hand her over.

There was no point trying to explain anything. Whoever or whatever Susannah Adderstone had been, it was a secret I would carry to my grave. I think perhaps her father guessed, but they would have believed him as little as me. Chief Inspector Raleigh was the only person who would have made sense of my story, but even he would have been powerless to stop the majestic process of the law. And he, of course, was dead.

I wonder if Rachel ever thinks of me. She is fourteen years old now, and I have heard that she lives with Tim's parents. They must be growing old. Soon, she will have no one again. Even when I come out of here, they are sure to stop me finding her. Unless she remembers, unless she comes to me of her own accord.

Richard Adderstone and I corresponded many times in the months before his death. There was one final surprise that he had been saving to the end. In one letter, I expressed bewilderment about one thing: that Sarah had been Susannah Trevorrow's double. His daughter had been directly related to Agnes, whom she resembled; that made a certain kind of sense. But Sarah, she had had no connection with any of them.

I fear you are wrong about your wife's unconnectedness, he wrote back. *As a matter of fact, her family are cousins of ours, if rather distant. They changed their name from Trevorrow to Trevor some time ago. Their branch of the family moved to the north of England around 1900. In time, they lost contact with their relatives. So it is not surprising that your wife had not the least suspicion of her Cornish origins. I have known about them for some time, of course. Family history is my hobby.*

He died six months later in his bed, cared for by a nurse. We never met face-to-face again. Some weeks later a letter arrived at the prison from Mr. Pentreath of Pentreath, Single, and Nesbitt. I was named a beneficiary in Richard Adderstone's will. By some legal contrivance, he had left Petherick House to me, as the next of kin surviving Sarah. It was not strictly within the terms of the entail, but under the circumstances no one quibbled. They weren't going to sell the house, after all.

It is quiet here. I think I am content. I do not understand what happened to my life, and I no longer want to understand. I have lived as intelligently and as gently as it has been possible for me to do. In the evenings I watch the shadows thicken beyond the bars on my window. My ghosts have all been laid to rest. In a few years I shall be a free man again. My flat has gone, every last penny eaten up by legal costs. My publishers tell me there is no hope of a second bite at the literary cherry. I shall be homeless and penniless. I have no choice, not really. The keys to Petherick House are waiting for me in a safe-deposit box in a bank in St. Ives. It will not seem a long journey this time.

Jonathan Aycliffe is a pseudonym for Daniel Easterman, the best-selling author of BROTHERHOOD OF THE TOMB, THE NINTH BUDDHA, and other thrillers. He was born in Ireland in 1949 and studied English, Persian, and Arabic at the Universities of Dublin, Edinburgh, and Cambridge. For several years he was a professor at Newcastle University. He currently lives in England with his wife.